Welcome to Jahannam

I0621673

Welcome to Jahannam

First Published in December 2016
Welcome to Jahannam Copyright 2016 Kit Cox
Cover design: Kit Cox
The moral rights of the author has been asserted

By the same author
Morningwood (2017)
Dr Tripps: Time Terror (2016)
Dr Tripps: Moon Monster (2016)
Smoke and Mirrors: The adventures of
Benjamin Gaul (2015)
The Monster Hunter: The adventures of
Benjamin Gaul (2014)
Dr Tripps: Kaiju Cocktail (2013)
How to bag a Jabberwock (2012)

Kit Cox

This book is dedicated to

The brave Men and Women of C.A.K.E;
who have travelled the Cosmos since 1847.

Welcome to Jahannam

Welcome to Jahannam
By Kit Cox

Chapter 1

There has always been talk of a history that flows throughout our own, one that hides in plain view and influences our religions, mythology, legends and dreams. A history not just of the worlds we know or of the universe we believe to stretch out ever expanding into the cosmos, but a shared history, perceived differently by all it touches on the many distant worlds of the myriad of hidden universes that spiral so close and unseen to our own.

It is a history of wars and monsters; of victories and heroes. It is a shared history - a union of dimensions. For all its difference it often remains the same, repeating patterns, like ripples on a pond.

Take the name Jack; it resonates with the Union-verse; a name for heroes, for monster hunters and giant killers; be you a Jack, Jacque or (I)ack (as the Celts would have it) then the Union-verse waits for you, plotting your adventures.

This however is the story of a James; a James whose mother married a Benjamin, who hailed from a long line of Benjamin's right back to a Benjamin who was a son of Jack, giving all his heirs the surname Jackson and still the Union-verse took notice.

James Jackson had experienced a happy childhood, and it had certainly been one of wonder. Fuelled by the stories of his mother, who assured him daily that he had come from a long line of adventurers, and that he carried a great weight on his shoulders to carry on that legacy. His father was happy to let the stories flow because he loved his wife with all of his heart. And what publican didn't like to hear the weaving of a good tale? It made your punters thirsty.

The adventurer's legacy was always held up to an element of reasonable doubt as his mother had no living, or at least "contactable family" to verify this bloodline, and his father never spoke of his seafaring past (before he settled to life as a publican) or of his ancestors. But if the doubts ever became too strong then his mother would counter happily with the fact that if his father had not swept her off her feet, then young James would have been the lucky offspring of a monster hunter, space explorer, time traveller or King. She was a good woman, as beautiful as she was funny, and if her stories tended towards the fantastical it was best to let them flow rather than question their validity just to see the sparkle in her eyes and hear the music of her laughter.

Kit Cox

The reality was that young James grew up with very little adventure in his life. Hidden away from it all in his father's inn, nestled close to the Limehouse district on an uneventful back street of London. It was a popular inn amongst the spice traders, sailors and dockworkers. It served a good line of ales, with clean rooms above for short term rent. James's father was a happy man; he ran a good trade from both his public and saloon bars and the rented rooms allowed a steady turnover of new faces. They had their regulars of course, brought in by either his father's listening ears or his mother's numerous skills and knowledge. Strange and varied folk would turn up at their door at all hours generally seeking his mother out for a whispered conversation or her famed ability to fix just about anything. In fact if his mother didn't have oil smudged somewhere on her, or if she wasn't sat hunched with a stranger, talking conspiratorially in the shadows of the bar, it had been a slow day.

The courtyard of the public house was so full of engines and boilers you could be easily mistaken for thinking you'd wandered into a scrap dealer's long before you realised you were in an old coaching house. As a boy, James would sit for hours and watch her work, asking her questions of the strangers who came by so often, always being directed instead into detailed descriptions of the task in which she

7

was currently undertaking, leaving the strangers and their stories a wonderfully undisclosed mystery.

So when it came time to find a trade of his own, James went the way of the mechanics apprentice rather than publican; which caused much more happiness to his father than it did to his mother. She was deeply bereft that her only child was to leave her, whereas his father was pleased that James saw publican as a job for later years when you wanted to settle and not the career of a young man full of life and adventure. It therefore came to pass that at the age of fifteen, James Jackson found himself apprenticed to one of his father's old regulars, a Mr Butteridge.

Mr Butteridge was a stocky man with neat whiskers and a good education. At first, under his tutorage, James was simply to watch others work and learn by observation, but quicker than expected it was discovered that the young lad was already quite adept at mechanics (after years of watching his mother at work) and he was given the upcoming trade of bicycles as his own little part of the Butteridge Empire of reliable repair. James loved being responsible for the machines that were becoming so popular and indispensible to the everyday lives of ordinary folk, and for many months he threw himself fully into the world of gears and chains.

8

However it was still a nice and welcome change when Mr Butteridge decided, on a whim, to start fixing the next big fad to come along; that of personal aeroplanes. Within this endeavour he felt it was something he needed an assistant for, and with James as the firm's only current apprentice he was the natural choice to help out.

The two of them would drive out in the works van to airfields around Kent and put the hobbies of rich men back together after they had inadvertently flown into the hay barn or an uncooperative tree (that had failed to move when screamed at.) Mr Butteridge would often joke with James that it took 500 bolts to put a plane together and just one carless nut to break it all across the countryside.

Soon Butteridge was making more money on fixing these hobby planes than on tending to tractors and steam engines, so he founded "Butteridge and Son Aeronautical Engineers" with James being elevated to the honorary position of the son, as the (unmarried and childless) Mr Butteridge said it scanned better on signage. The duo continued to drive around expanding their territory to encompass the whole country, rescuing aircraft from the inexpert hands of landed gentry. James was lucky enough during these visits, to be taught how to fly by one of the more regular customers. A funny cove by the moniker of Lord Percy. Mr Butteridge saw Lord Percy as a

Welcome to Jahannam

close friend, despite the fact the man was always up to no good. Butteridge overlooked Percy's short fallings as he saw the lessons he gave as valuable to the company's trade and he was a lot happier with the boy taking to the skies than himself. However after teaching James to pilot various aircraft, Lord Percy took it upon himself to announce all of his future repairs (of which there were likely to be many) were now free of labour costs as payment for his time and expertise in the boy's instruction. James had to admit that he didn't mind a bit as he could now take to the clouds and experience the thrill of the vehicles he worked upon, understanding them better than he ever had before. Butteridge however, saw it as a cheek to announce this hidden cost to what he had seen as a favour from a friend and took it upon himself to find as many ways as possible to not be available when repairs were needed at the Percy Estate.

It was under these conditions of master and apprentice that James found that he had been working on planes for a couple of years when the war started. It didn't take long before the Allies were in the skies over the trenches of Europe, the observational and then tactical advantages of the plane being recognised instantly as a leap in modern warfare. All the young men were leaving home to defend the nation and James was just as headstrong and proud to do the same. He was looking to join the infantry and get in at the front of the fighting but instead, on a twist of fate he signed up for the Royal Flying Corps the very moment he knew he could. With his background in aviation he was accepted without delay.

Being found to be an experienced mechanic, rather than a full time pilot, it was agreed without James's full consent that he would be fixing rather than flying and although he tried his hardest to keep it hidden he couldn't have been more annoyed. James had certainly always had a streak of egotism running through him and had secretly bought into all of mother's talk of adventurer's blood in his veins. He had wanted to be up in the skies, not just as a jolly flyboy winning over the ladies hearts but as a skilled pilot who wanted to prove himself a hero and come home as a decorated Ace. He certainly didn't want to be a nameless grease monkey, however important he knew the job was.

So when he found out they were recruiting for pilots, he stole one of the planes in for repairs and crashed the party -quite literally as it would turn out - and next to all the nervous first timers in from their country estates he was a star. It should therefore not be a surprise that his egotism got the better of him and he truly wanted to show how much more advanced he was than the other pilots that day. In his eagerness to shine out he quite forgot that the plane he was flying was a borrowed one with an unknown and unrepaired fault.

It had also become known to all present (from passed whispers) that seasoned airmen were currently watching these test flights and the actions of that day were more than likely to become the origins of any nicknames that would stay with the young pilots forever. With that thought in his mind and a burning egotism in his heart James thought he would fly like an experienced Ace and then all who were watching would be impressed with the supposed novice's skills and he would be naturally known as Ace or some such accolade before shooting even a single shot in battle. His subsequent showboating impressed everyone on the ground with its daring and precision control, except for maybe the watching commanders who frowned on that sort of thing but more importantly it also failed to impress the damaged plane that James had purloined from the hanger earlier that day. Soon the aircraft chose to show its own discomfort not with tuts like the officers but instead with a more serious broken axle, technically leaving the young pilot without wheels to land. Unfortunately for James, with the sound of the engine and because of the positioning of the damage he was unaware of the danger and taxied in as normal, believing the waved arms of spectators to just be exuberant adulations at his acrobatics.

It wasn't the flying of that day that impressed but instead the skill James exhibited on landing , skills that had allowed him to walk away fairly unscathed and with enough of a plane left to repair, skills that had moved him from the grease pit to the pilot's quarters.

It had also been true that other airman had watched the flights with interest and from that moment forward, despite initial protest, James Jackson had been known as Crash.

Welcome to Jahannam

Chapter 2

War, as you can imagine was hell. By the time "Crash" was in a plane above the trenches the gentlemanly waves had been replaced with Dogfights and he quickly learned far too many young men never made it to the end of their first month. Crash apparently had luck on his side and despite being shot down twice he was always closer to friend than foe whilst in the great muddy wastes of no man's land. It was always the plane that took the brunt of the damage (although of course he didn't remain scar free.)

***

It was the morning Crash had been waiting for; confirmation of his fifth (and hopefully sixth) confirmed kills in sky combat. He already had four confirmations under his belt and a couple of question marks (there were always doubts in big dog fights about who had fired the killing rounds or if the crash was pilot error) but that morning he knew one hundred percent he had downed two more German fighters; a feat he had completed single headedly on a routine evening flight. He just had to wait on the officials' tent for a confirmation and the much sought after gaining of Ace status awarded for five or more confirmed enemy kills. Crash was already a Captain, a rank gained solely from his long service record as opposed to conduct befitting an officer, so it was the justified adulation and boasting rights of Ace that he craved more than anything as he had earned them fair and square.

It was in his eagerness to hear the news that he had taken a chair and sat himself down outside the mess tent, completely unaware of how his positioning was about to lead to a series of events that would change his life. Although distracted he could not help but notice the two officers that approached. At this time of the morning many airmen came to get something to eat; taking the chance to fill their bellies for the day, unsure if they would get chance again. However, it was unusual for high ranking officers to chow down with the common men and low rankers so the approach of the two men was a notable difference to the day.

Crash of course knew them both by name and reputation but was unaware either of them knew him until he was addressed.

"Captain Jackson, go find your crate. You're going up." The first said with the clarity of an officer not used to being second guessed. "I went up last night Sir." Crash responded his eyes not leaving the administration tent so not noticing that the unguarded words caused the lead officer to stop suddenly in his tracks, almost resulting in a comedy collision with his comrade.

"I'm sorry!" The officer said; without turning to look at Crash "I wasn't aware I was giving out invitations to a party that I hoped your lordship might be able to attend."

Crash knew the calm tone, and without another thought snapped to his feet with a smart salute. No more words were needed. The officers moved into the mess tent to press gang more volunteers and Crash with a final longing look towards the admin tent went begrudgingly in search of his biplane.

***

It turned out that the morning's mission was to guard a single observation balloon, which had been anchored only the day before. It was getting good information, but its presence was obvious to anyone with a telescope or pair of field binoculars. Despite this disadvantage however, high command had instructed it was to stay perilously situated for as long as possible and that they would scramble an armed airborne guard. To the royal flying corps it was a babysitting duty, which no one liked, but in this instance it certainly had a greater chance of engagement so volunteers had apparently been easy to find.

The mission was clear; intercept and destroy any enemies of the observation craft, preferably on their way to their destination rather than on their way back home. Timing was clearly everything and the squadron was scrambled.

***

Crash always loved the drone of the squadron with its mixed engines as they took to the air and found formation; to his ears it was a sound beautiful to hear - full of melody and depth. He took the time to look around to find who he was in the skies with, and was greeted by a swarm of regimented planes of different nations and design, mostly French pilots but a smattering of British and one double seat craft complete with cheery Canadians. He always waved to the British pilots and Canadians because they waved back but the French would either just nod or not acknowledge at all, very much like the Germans. In fact if you were unsure if a plane was friend or foe it was wise to wave; if they waved back they were certainly on your team, if they didn't then you had to fly defensively until they did or didn't start shooting.

Everyone in their cockpits was wrapped up warm that day. The morning sky was chill and full of low cloud meaning the balloon would be obscured for the most part, but they had flown with good map references to a definitive and anchored point. This meant that despite the poor visibility, the Allied planes were soon all circling their precious balloon.

Welcome to Jahannam

It was larger than most observation balloons and almost spherical, rather that the elongated sacks of most observation platforms. This platform was attached to the balloon above by climbable rigging and appeared to be an armoured box with presumably soldiers hunkered down inside, seizing any break in the cloud to observe enemy positions and send telegrams back to the ground. Only one heavy chain held the craft anchored to the spot far below and this in turn protected the important telegraph wires from enemy attack or unfavourable weather conditions, but despite its altitude and the gentle winds the balloon didn't appear to move, remaining fixed in place as if the chain itself was a solid unwavering tower upon which it sat.

As he flew past Crash watched the canvas of the balloon being buffeted for a moment, reminded briefly of the canvas his mother would cover secret projects in the yard with back home, before turning his attention back to the task at hand.

The heavy cloud was successfully muffling the sound of any approaching German squadron, and Crash always found something comical about a group of allied planes moving in perfect formation whilst the pilots contained within were all spinning around in their cockpits, looking in every direction like children searching for friends to come and play.

They needn't have worried because only a few moment later their playmates broke above the clouds, a group almost as big as their own; comprised chiefly of the over decorated German Albatross Biplanes but strangely with one larger observation plane at their core, clearly wishing to exploit the observational area the allied balloon was finding so favourable.

The command was of course to dive and engage and it was one in which they took no hesitation, as German pilots were often far superior and skilled when given time to think.

The resulting engagement was immediate and as chaotic as any Crash had ever participated in. The rhythmic beat of the Vickers machine guns filled the air, clearly heard over the rising and falling throb of Bentley engines, as planes danced like lethal ballerinas across the heavens. At one point Crash found he had become engaged with a bright yellow biplane, falling in behind his quarry as it tried to shake him, following as tightly as he could, holding back on pointless shots which would only make his opponent more skittish and less likely to fall in as a firm target. Crash was therefore surprised when the plane in front opened fire. He swung out to remove it as an obstruction to his sight line and evaluated what its target was and there before them was the balloon. The shots tore through the canvas and it ripped open, billowing out like

Welcome to Jahannam

a flag. In a normal situation it would be now that the observation platform and chain should fall like a rock...but it inexplicably just hung there. The two planes shot by the balloon, both banking to do so, avoiding the loose canvas as they went. Crash saw that beneath the ruined cover was a metal and wood sphere that had no business staying aloft, canvas covered or not. To Crash's eyes it was as solid and unmoving as a packing crate on the London docks. He couldn't quite believe what he was seeing, but in a heartbeat he was past and the details were lost to him. He turned his attention quickly back to the yellow plane before him, and engaged both guns. He did not know what he had seen, but he was sure command would not wish the Germans to have seen it either.

The pitched battle took Crash's full attention and he had not taken time to focus on the angriness of the clouds that gathered around them. That is until lightning tore apart the sky and dark heavy rain fell suddenly, hammering the wings of his craft.

It certainly wasn't flying weather, and it had come from nowhere. Soon the winds were as bad as they could be and visibility had become a luxury. He didn't want to lose his foe but Crash realised he needed to concentrate on the weather not the fight, and hoped his enemy would be thinking the same. He wrestled with his angry controls as best he could, finding that his plane seemed to have become alive with the power of nature, possessed by the spirit of a wild beast as it bucked and reared across the swell of the storm. Crash caressed the dash of his trusty Sopwith as if trying to control a skittish steed, convinced it was going to shake itself apart with each violent gust. All the while he was eager to part from the clutches of the tempest and find his yellow enemy again.

A recognition of sound over the storm made Crash glance up from his controls to see the dark shape of another plane approaching through the cloud. With the familiar drone of the enemies' Albatross engine, his former prey had either turned back or been flipped about by the storm, and now they were on the same path in opposite directions. He had no way of avoiding a collision and he hoped briefly the universe was looking out for him. As his thoughts almost strayed into prayer they were rudely interrupted; as if from nowhere a third plane joined the party, rising with such unnatural speed that it certainly must have been propelled by some unseen force greater than its engines a phenomena often attributed to storms, and all three pilots realised the very real threat of a triple and explosive impact. Crash instinctively threw his arms across his face sensing the unavoidable moment. The protective action meant he released his controls and left the storm to decide his movements,

Welcome to Jahannam

which resulted in his plane banking sharply and away from the collision. The racing ascent however brought the third plane into the path of the oncoming yellow Albatross and the two exploded in a great ball of fire, sending forth a concussive blast that spun Crash and his plane, pushing them further out of the path of serious harm. The heat brought Crash back to his senses and he grabbed sharply back for his joystick, trying to level the Sopwith against its giddying spin and the raging storm that battered it. The ferocity of the explosion raced outwards with tremendous force clearing the clouds and charring some of the paint off of Crashes plane and singeing his hair and flight jacket. As Crash plummeted he cursed as a wing cable broke under the strain and he suddenly lost all worthwhile control left to him. The defence of a solitary balloon had taken a perilous and weird turn, but it was about to get weirder still.

Crash broke beneath the clouds and pulled back on his joystick as hard as his muscles would allow, but to little avail. His plane ploughed into the thick churned mud of no man's land with an impact that sent hot oil and cold earth in a great wave across the jarred pilot within.

As the pain of the impact filtered into his bones Crash coughed and spluttered, before being brought back to his senses again by the rain of burning debris that fell around him; an aftermath of the collision above. He unbuckled fast pulling himself from the cockpit, and with practiced skill he flung himself into the dark wet soil that embraced his downed craft. His only thought was to get away from his oil soaked wreckage as quick as possible to avoid the ever present chance that the flaming debris would ignite his crashed plane with him in the blast zone. He ran and stumbled away, falling onto his face many times before finally disorientation took hold and he fell forwards into the mud spent and breathless, before slowly rolling over to look back towards his stricken plane. The ground around it burnt but the plane itself remained doused only in wet soil, free from further damage. For a moment Crash believed it could be rescued with the right amount of horses to pull it from the sticky mud and pull it back home, but when something immense crashed down upon it the plane was lost in an instant and the flames extinguished.

Crash half expected the falling solid sphere of the balloon to have been the downfall of his stricken craft but as he looked up he was stunned into silence. Looming above the fallen pilot was an immense creature, its foot planted firmly where his plane had once sat. The storm itself seemed to be moving in, concentrating its intensity on the gigantic form, like a swarm of bees closing in on a honey raiding bear. The beast, for beast it certainly was, thrashed about

in the turmoil and Crash realised it held tightly
in one of its hands the Canadian plane as if it
was a toy. The pilot was gone but the gunner's
body flopped about like a doll. Then with no
care for what it held, the creature flung the
plane like a rock into the tempest and Crash
was suddenly aware what had propelled the
plane earlier, flung with such unnatural speed
up through the clouds to impact with his enemy
and save him from death. Around its other arm
was tangled the securing chain of the balloon,
and as it thrashed about the solid sphere
whipped about like a medieval morning star.
Crash retreated as the sphere carved a deep
trench through the mud, the force tearing the
armoured box from its underside. Freed of the
weight it went climbing rapidly skyward
coming to a shuddering halt, held fast by the
entangled chain like a fairground balloon tied to
the wrist of a young child by a careful parent.
Crash picked himself up and started to run
towards the armoured box and perceived safety
within, to be safely shielded from the rage of
the beast. With his sudden movement though,
the creature seemed to sense his presence and
dipped its misshapen head down towards him.
The great maw like mouth opened wide to
reveal impossible rows of needle sharp teeth
and bone crushing molars. It let out a tortured
roar before turning back into the circling storm.

The storms noise grew in intensity as if in response to the rising of the creature's anger. Thunder rumbled louder than any of the ranks of massed artillery and lighting crackled through the swirling clouds earthing on the creatures body, both lighting and obscuring it in equal measures. Then with a clap of thunder so loud that it moved the mud around Crash like water, the storm and the creature were gone. Crash laid panting and alone in the slime, the warm morning sun beating down on his body.

With time he moved stumbling and dazed to the armoured box and franticly forced open its cover. Inside, the observation platform was a shambles; maps, photography equipment and field phone in disarray from the impact but thankfully and surprisingly unmanned.

Welcome to Jahannam

Chapter 3

Ironically, true monsters had no place in war and no one believed the tale.

Within days Captain James "Crash" Jackson was honourably discharged from active service. He was put into a Military hospital safe in his home county of Kent, comfortably set up to recover from his trauma at full government expense. It was discussed many times with Crash by various experts that shell shock had lead to the delusions he experienced and should have been expected after such a long service at the front. The final injustice to Crash was that his last two combat kills were never again discussed and the honour of Ace was never rested upon his shoulders. He was destined to become a broken man sitting unknown and unrecognised in a wicker chair overlooking well maintained gardens.

His mother and father visited often. Despite their son's reluctance to communicate, his mother enthusiastically tried to make him see that he wasn't mistaken, that there was more in the world than people talked about. However, despite her effort Crash refused to rise from his malaise and she was eventually hushed by his father who told her to let the boy be to recover in his own time.

Just under a month after his discharge, the war ended and a fragile peace settled over the world.

It was a warm autumn afternoon when the nurses disappeared inside to listen to the gramophone, spirits were high and Crash was left in the garden with just his thoughts.

"May I sit?" a voice interrupted, as the backing of jazz was hushed by a closing door.

Crash turned to see an elderly grey haired lady, dressed smartly in tweeds in the style of the country set, stood beside the empty chair next to where he sat.

"It's a free country." Crash answered before turning back to the view.

"Well it certainly is now." said the Lady sitting down. "Well, at least in appearance."

The two sat quietly, but the closeness of the stranger made Crash uncomfortable and he turned briefly to look at her. He was surprised to find he was already being appraised by the glamorous older lady with rouged cheeks and pursed lips.

"I knew your mother well." The woman began her conversation as if it was not unusual to be studying another human being "She was our mechanic back in the day."

"She was a lot of people's mechanic." Crash found himself answering, surprised at his own abrupt rudeness.

Welcome to Jahannam

The woman nodded sagely "A good job too. Your mother could make a table purr if she was given enough time to tinker. However, she was our mechanic before she met your father. Cut her teeth so to speak, mending the things we found all too easy to break. Do you mind if I smoke?" Without waiting for an answer she produced a slim silver case, removed a tailor made cigarette which she elegantly placed between her deep red lips, and lit.

Crash waved away the offer of taking one for himself. He suddenly found the revelation of a past employer of his mother an intriguing aside from the view and he turned to face the woman better.

"The thing is," she continued, "she did it as a favour. The chance of a new life, doing something she loved.... and although she felt she owed us, over the years we became more in her debt than she ever was in ours." She smiled a warm smile at Crash. "I believe your story young man, and more importantly so do my colleagues. We're looking for a pilot to test fly an experimental aircraft. It's currently all hush hush but time is a factor and I think you'd be perfect for the job and it would go a long way to us paying back your Mother if you said yes." Crash shook his head slightly "I'm sorry. What story exactly is it you believe?"

The woman looked very serious "The fact you saw and interacted with a one of our other craft,

over the battlefields of Europe. On the very day
it was taken by some creature with my
Daughter and Son in law on board"

Crash didn't break eye contact with the
woman. It felt like a test was being set - besides
his mother no one talked about the incident.
This was a friend of hers and about the same
age, so it could easily be a stupid set up to push
him from his depression. A lifeline of hope to
cling to.

"One of your craft?" he asked finally making
sure not to add any more information to the
conversation.

"We've been working out of the Kent area for
over fifty years; as I said your mother worked
for us. Actually, with us is more accurate.
During her time with us she added a sense of
national pride to our little setup and so when the
war came along we thought we'd do our bit;
offered up our unique craft as observational
platforms." She took a long draft of the
cigarette and blew out a swirling cloud of grey
blue smoke "Kept well clear of the fighting
though. We were a civilian unit. Happy to do
our part but not happy to end others lives or
endanger our own. That was the deal and the
ministry snapped it up. Seems we weren't as
secret as we had thought, at least in certain
circles."

"Your craft were the observational
platforms?" Crash asked again adding the extra

information.

"They were indeed. Not all of them you understand as most were proper balloons, subject to the constraints of air pressure and wind. Ours of course were disguised as balloons as the general consensus was that it was a technology the enemy didn't have, and they didn't want them to have. So we did our bit and in the process of non engagement we lost one and her crew." She stopped to take another drag of her cigarette and dabbed her eyes with a handkerchief. "I read your report. I read all the reports of the incident before they went into the incinerator and we were left to pick up the pieces. I would have been in mourning now, along with countless others, if that had been the end of it.

A few days ago we got a radio signal, a single beacon telling us that not only were they alive and well but with enough instruction contained within that we could locate exactly where they were."

Crash sat up "You've found them; they can confirm my story?" He asked realising how hopeful and possibly selfish he sounded.

She half smiled at Crash "We've certainly found them. "She paused as if fighting emotions "We just can't get to them."

Crash slumped back in his chair, and then the initial words of the conversation started to seep in. He turned back to the woman "You want me to go and get them don't you? It's not that they can't be got, it's just you don't currently have the skill and you somehow think I might."

The woman simply nodded. Crash thought longer, trying to concentrate on the words the woman had spoken; he had started to lose the knack of listening since the war, each day disappearing a bit more into himself. The woman was watching him as he thought and ran the conversation back through his head. She didn't interrupt, but lit another cigarette and put the first out beneath her heel.

"They're not here anymore are they? That creature... it dragged them somewhere else?"

The woman nodded again then cleared her throat "It was the storm that took them, not the creature. The storm was for the creature, they just got hooked up and dragged along for the ride. And they weren't the first."

Crash sat back again, this time thinking clearer. When he spoke it was more to the air around him "Mother often speaks of other worlds, existing alongside our own, little pocket kingdoms. She says she's visited a few."

The woman seemed to let out a small laugh "I don't know about that, but with your mother and her friends anything is possible. This isn't another world...well it is but in the more traditional sense. This is another planet."

Welcome to Jahannam

It was Crash's turn to laugh. He couldn't help but glance up at the autumn sky. "Now I know why no one wanted to believe my story. I barely believe yours, and I saw it with my own eyes."

"We've been visiting the cosmos for generations now. Our craft, like the one you saw over the trenches, defy gravity and can take our explorations beyond the pull of this planet and out into the stars. We are the Futurenauts, Captain Jackson, and we need your skill to retrieve my family."

Crash turned back to the woman "I'm a pilot not a... futurenaut. I can't be what you need. I have to fight gravity at every turn. You must be the masters of it. "

The woman laughed again "I'm telling you this all so candidly because already people don't believe your stories. You have to believe that we are not the masters of Gravity; if anything we understand it less than most because our float crews strive to remove it from their calculations. Our craft are not affected by its pull until we need to be, we drift until we wish to be dragged back down. We reach the planets by their call to us, once grounded we are as flightless as a Dodo. We need a pilot, someone who can fight that pull."

Crash was confused. "Can't you just do that

again; let your futurenauts travel to the planet your family have been dragged to, in the way you already do? I respect your desire to help my mother return her son's sanity back to the world but it strikes me you already have a far better prepared crew at hand."

The woman pointed at the sun. "If it was not for that great burning beast in the heavens then I would have done just that. The planet we need to reach rests perpetually behind the sun and its gravitational drag will forever hamper our rescue. Captain Jackson you understand enough to not need to be convinced that our mission is not the folly of a grieving mother, but you are also not our only hope. What you currently are, is a faster solution than the alternative."

Crash knew enough to question the facts presented to him, his father had taught him that. He was also aware that questioning the perceived facts would often lead to answers you had to have an open mind to accept, his mother had taught him that. So he continued. "No planet lies behind the sun forever. I've seen an orrery and we all spiral in and out of sight of each other. You just need a good telescope to pinpoint when a planet is in the heavens. Why can you not simply wait until that time comes to pass?"

The woman smiled "I'm impressed. You know more than I thought you would about the

Welcome to Jahannam

distant sky and its workings. You are of course right, the planets we observe we do so because we can see them when conditions allow, but this planet follows an orbit so similar to our own it will remain hidden from Earth for many lifetimes. We may indeed one day have chance to glimpse it, and it may have appeared in the heavens before but it is too infrequent and dangerous to steer our craft in its direction by its pull alone. This planet we need to fly to, fighting the sun's pull along the way, if we stand any chance of getting there with haste and saving my family. If we fail to find a willing pilot then our Futurenauts can skip from planet to planet with the craft we have but I fear for their safety in such an exercise. This is a rescue with a time limit and we need you Captain Jackson." The woman took Crash's hand in hers and he could see from her eyes the honesty of her words.

The moment was interrupted by a nurse opening the door to the veranda, the building sounds of a jazz solo echoing behind her. "Are you okay Captain Jackson?" she asked kindly, not out of true concern but in the scripted way they often did just before rounds. Crash smiled back at the nurse.
"I believe I am. Is it possible to bring me my suitcase, I think I am going on a journey."
**

Only a few short days later Crash Jackson was back in uniform, all be it a civilian uniform with its smart naval blue jacket complete with patches, tight beige jodhpurs and patent leather riding boots. His life had purpose, direction and aircraft. Lots of beautiful, unfathomable aircraft. They mostly sat stock still, wonderfully chained down spheres, but some bobbed like bubbles defying gravity and although new to his eyes they already had a history far older than his time on this Earth.

He had grown up around Kent and had no idea of the deep and secretive history of the Romney Marshes and their program of space exploration. He enquired excitedly about how it had remained secret with such ease and was answered simply.

"Very little we do will actually happen here. It all happens out there, and we get there by the shortest route every time."

The spheres, it transpired, were made by an application of a substance called Cavorite - a branded solution manufactured by a single British company. It wasn't uniquely supplied to this organisation Crash was surprised to discover, there were more Cavorite affiliates around the world, but in this case it was responsible for the adorable anachronism for which this organisation were known.

Welcome to Jahannam

"C.A.K.E "

Or to give them their full title "the Cavorite Affiliation of Kentish Explorers"

***

Despite the name, which didn't really stand up against the Royal flying Corps, Crash was proud to be part of team of men and woman who still had the spirit of adventure in their hearts, and his story was not only being believed but was also being backed up with evidence and fact.

An aerial photo of his downed plane surfaced and clearly showed it was crushed in a giant footprint. The investigation didn't stop there, and eventually photos and varied documents filled the C.A.K.E offices until the only conversation was of the weird storms; storms that seemed to seek out the even weirder giants.

It was decided the information was key to the safety of a rescue mission so was hastily put together in a field book and passed along the chain of command.

***

"Titans: A Guide." Crash read aloud, picking the book up and turning instantly to the first illustration.

"It's going to be invaluable to you Captain Jackson." The woman before him said whilst watching the pilot scan the pages.

"Why?" Crash enquired looking up into the

face of the lady from his hospital who he now knew as Lady Belle.

"...Because you may encounter any one of these during your rescue." She added calmly

Crash just laughed "Some of these are thousands of years old. "

"You need to become an expert in Titans, Captain Jackson. That doesn't just mean looking out the window and reacting; you need to study the classics. Know your enemy. I refuse to send you to a planet we have no information on with just hope, when we clearly know it has been a dumping ground for these creatures for historical generations" Lady Belle didn't smile as she spoke and Crash knew not to make jokes.

"Why now?" was all he could think to enquire. "Because your craft is ready, and because of limited time you will only be able to test out its capabilities as you travel."

"Can I see her?" Crash asked hopefully.
***

Stood in the hanger, Crash was dressed in the uniform C.A.K.E had issued; allowing a level of comfort, tradition and pride to radiate throughout his posture. His tussled, chestnut hair was held fairly secure by the band of his flight goggles and a light breeze through the open doors moved the warming fur of the flight jacket he had slipped on. Today he planned to be the poster child for all things forward thinking, heroic and aeronautical, but if a camera man had been present he would have marvelled less at the stoic officer and a lot more at the air craft behind him.

Sat on specially crafted crab-like legs was a vehicle of pure mechanical brilliance and sculpted design. The artistically rendered and burnished chrome body honouring the latest Art Deco movement, to the point that the whole vehicle looked more like a sculpture than an aircraft and was far removed from the elegant simplicity of the Cavorite spheres.

The central part of the vehicle was still the sphere, there was no reason to redesign a perfected classic, although the sphere was larger and the impact buffers had been removed to allow the additional parts to be fitted. Around the circumference of the central sphere, a sculpted skirt had been installed, with two great propellers recessed into the surface on either side. The skirt appeared to float independently of the sphere and Crash realised it would be able to move freely around the central body and if positioned just right the propellers angle could easily power away from whatever pulled the craft close. If he was to be unkind to its design it would be to describe it as an upturned saucer with a cricket ball through its centre but in all honesty he simply couldn't be unkind because she was magnificent.

"She's a beaut." Crash said with a whistle. Causing an overly clean mechanic to look up from his work and come over.

"She's certainly something isn't she. "

"How does the skirt connect?" Crash asked out of genuine mechanical interest.

"Good question. Technically the sphere and skirt are separate. Think of it as a safety feature, if the skirt goes wrong for any reason you can jettison and fly the sphere in the traditional way, although without buffers the landing may be rough but it's better than being sucked into the sun. The skirt is treated in Cavorite too and held to the sphere by magnets, the propellers will allow you to fly in any atmosphere and also travel through liquid but in the vacuum of space they will eject a propellant that should in theory thrust you forward. You only really need to use the propellers in gravity situations or for course adjustment, thus saving your battery power by spending most of your time flying like a classic sphere whilst in space." The Mechanic was clearly happy with the design but Crash's mechanic brain was kicking in too.

"She's electric. Are batteries the best form of energy? Won't they just power down used or not?"

The mechanic sucked his teeth holding back his annoyance at any hint of imperfection

Welcome to Jahannam

"She's built for distance and speed. You're not supposed to be spinning about the sky having a dog fight in her. Besides, when you are being pulled through space the outer skirt is designed to spin and charge the batteries like a dynamo." The Mechanic suddenly looked like a proud father not prepared to let the brash young beau take his daughter to the dance.

"Sorry! I didn't mean to offend, she's a beauty and finding her quirks will be half the fun and just one more reason to fall in love." He smiled at the mechanic "Does she have a name?" and this simple question seemed to win the man back over

"Well technically she's just an experiment - a one off - so we hadn't thought much about naming her beyond what she could do. On her paperwork she's the slingshot." He paused as if not sure for a moment if he should share his next thought with the handsome captain, the old school days of the intellectuals being bullied by the sports team was coming back to the mechanic but as soon as he looked over at Crash admiring the ship, that fear fled his mind and he continued "but I think that sounds like a brutish kids toy and she's just far too elegant. So I like to call her Harmony due to how she all holds together."

Crash jutted his jaw forward and gave a pleased nod of his head "I like it. Harmony she is then."

This seemed to appease the mechanic further and finally smiling again he patted the skirt "Look, I understand your worries about her batteries but she's built well and as long as you make sure they stay out of the red you'll be fine." he looked back at Crash. "We do have another outfit for you to wear though whilst you're in space, just in case."

***

Crash was pleased to find the outfit fitted over most of his original clothes. It was a one piece, blue in colour but under the red landing lights of the hanger it was taking on a purple hue suggesting the fabric had been treated in some way, possibly fire retardant. It was light, but the extra leather webbing that held the more practical parts in place gave it weight. Crash now had secured on his shoulders the neck part of the breathing helmet that he was to wear during flight, with its ridged breathing tube leading to a compact breathing apparatus on his belt. On his back was a device that looked like an air tank but remained unattached to the helmet. Crash carried the hardened glass dome that would complete the look under his left arm, whilst admiring the C.A.K.E patch sewn onto his right.

"Well you certainly look the part." Lady Belle intoned, bringing Crash from his self admiration.

"Thank you." He answered. "The float crew

Welcome to Jahannam

explained where I'm going I may not have a breathable atmosphere, so I may have to wear this" he tapped the dome. "The backpack I've been reliably informed is an experimental parachute if the slingshot happens to fail and I have to bail out: it works in both zero and high gravity. I threw the rest of my things in a duffel bag just in case I do get caught out; doesn't help to be wandering the countryside dressed as a comic book alien." Crash laughed.

"Just be careful Captain Jackson. This is an experimental craft and your mission is important. Not just to your life, but to others too." She gave these words a moment to sink in before proceeding "Do you have a flight path?"

"Yes Ma'am! I'm all set, aim for the big bright thing in the sky then at the last minute spin around the back and head for Earth two. The moment I break through its atmosphere I'll be following the beacon." Crash said with practiced confidence.

"You understand all your instruments?" She asked, more out of duty than concern.

"Yes Ma'am! The science division have gone over every instrument with me and I have been allowed to dismantle and reassemble several to allow for calibration and fixing in the field."

"Are you happy to take her out Captain?" She said, looking at the aircraft with a sceptical eye. "Yes Ma'am! I want to see what's she's capable of." He paused for a moment "If it goes wrong. Tell my mother I went out doing what I love, not sitting on a veranda. My blood just wouldn't allow the latter."

"I will do and I understand you are taking a huge risk for us. We do appreciate everything you're doing Captain. Float control has only given you a one hour window for her launch so if you're ready, now is the time."
Crash saluted "Thank you Ma'am! I won't let you down."

She smiled back with no salute, reminding Crash he was no longer in the military (despite the uniforms they all wore) then with little fuss they parted. Crash walked back over to the Slingshot, realising he was already thinking of her as Harmony.
"Hello Girl. Permission to come abroad?" he whispered before ducking beneath her skirt and opening the hidden round hatch beneath the sphere.

The interior was large and comfortable looking (designed to take up to four people). It had a reclined area with enough space to leave the cockpit seat, rest up, and have something to eat, maybe even go over the guides he had yet to read in full. It was to be his home for awhile and already Crash could see it becoming a

Welcome to Jahannam

restful nook and the thought of sleeping whilst in the weightlessness of space filled him with the same boyish glee he used to get from camping out in the back yard among his mother's repairs.

He moved into the sculpted leather seat of the cockpit, checked his helmet was secured and through the domed front window gave the ground crew the thumbs up. He was pleased to see the maiden flight had brought out most of the techs and crew to watch. They all knew that in theory she would fly but secrecy had meant this was her first time up, and as well as carrying out his rescue mission Crash had to monitor and report back on the craft so others could be built with any needed improvements.

The controls were familiar to crash as he had spent a good amount of time practicing on the simulator (a room set up like the crafts interior) so even now he flipped switches like an old pro. The sound of the hydraulics pulling the legs up however was new and Crash couldn't help but let out a glee filled laugh as the Harmony began to hover, only restrained from full flight by its heavy anchor, it shifted slightly as it found it's true gravitational level. Some of the gathered ground crew step nervously back, allowing Crash to see a prominent countdown board, as it flipped the numbers down from 10 and Crash braced for the release of the anchor.

9,8,7,6,

He checked his helmet again

5, 4,3,2,1

the release was breathtaking for both the crew and the pilot. Anything not held securely in the hanger tried to leave with Harmony, with some paperwork being quite successful in its escape as the craft flew directly upwards through the circular opening in the roof and into the air.

She shot skywards as straight as an arrow and in moments was out of sight of the ground crew; there was a moment of silence and then a great cheer filled the room

"Another successful launch Ma'am." Said a female float controller smiling as Lady Belle finally took her eyes of the clouds above the launch pad and looked at her.

"Just make sure we keep him safe. Captain Jackson is one of ours now."

***

Inside the cockpit Crash really was breathless. Not out of excitement, but from the fact he couldn't get his lungs to inflate against the pressure of the sudden inertia. He was in danger of blacking out during his very first launch. He scrabbled at his helmet apparatus and found a release valve he should have deployed sooner and with a quick twist his helmet filled once more with air, the pressure

Welcome to Jahannam

pushing into his lungs and inflating them again, making Crash gasp like a drowning man breaking the surface.

What a rush, his heart was pounding his head was dizzy and Harmony suddenly felt as light as a feather. Outside the grey Autumnal air grew darker and then for a blinding second there was light filling the cockpit before a perfect vista of stars filled the view. This time his breath was taken away by sheer beauty.

He must have floated for a bit before he couldn't help but give in to his desire to roll the beautiful skirt about the outer shell of the sphere and with a slight twitch of the stick, the responsive equipment rolled and spun. The whoop of delight Crash let out was amazing, this baby could fly.

<<Having fun Captain Jackson>> the almost mechanical voice of the radio filled the cockpit as his float control operator spoke for the first time, and Harmony suddenly had a female voice.

"It's glorious. The take off was smooth as silk." Crash replied realising instantly he was using his flirting voice, despite having no idea what the operator looked like.

<<That's grand news Captain. Can you please radio link your instruments so we can monitor you?>>

Crash looked at his bank of controls and flicked

up three switches.

"You should be getting data any moment, Control."

There was a lengthy pause allowing Crash to enjoy the speed he was travelling and the slow realisation of weightlessness as he moved out of the planets grip.

<<Thank you Captain, we are starting to receive you. >>

"I'm going to do a few manoeuvres with the propellers whilst I'm still close to Earth and a bit of gravitational force, give the tech boys something to work on straight away and then I'm going to head out towards the Sun. Might as well start off somewhere big and normally off limits, now I've been given the chance to explore space." Crash finally looked back at the Earth as he spoke, it was still filling most of the view but the curvature was obvious and what had once been contours on a map was now a very real image; it took his breath away for a third time.

<<It's beautiful isn't It.>> the voice said after a pause

"So beautiful." Crash responded almost dreamily before asking with more focus "Have you seen it?"

<<Many times Captain but It never fails to look magnificent.>> Again Crash was left with his thoughts for a moment before the radio spoke again

Welcome to Jahannam

<<Do you wish to try the propellers now Captain? >> The voice questioned and Crash was snapped away from the view and back to his controls.

"I certainly think it's for the best, and please call me Crash; I'm not in the military now." he suggested with the flirty tone returning to his voice.

<< If you'd like to go ahead then I shall monitor from here Cap... Crash.>> the voice said and Crash grinned as he thought he heard a faint implication of a smile to the words.

***

The propeller test went without hitch, the electric engines and the propellant release made a wonderfully tuneful hum rather than the throaty throb of the Bentley engines he was used to, and dipping Harmony back into the embrace of the Earth he noticed the noise simply became more insistent as if actually having to work harder against the pull. The added gravity on the craft was also allowing Crash to pull off some wonderfully tight turns and quick manoeuvres; although he was aware one or two were a little too quick and/or tight and he felt slightly sick and dizzy, which led to the realisation that Harmony was more robust and manoeuvrable than him, but with tests done and float control happy he was back off into space and onto the mission at hand.

    <<Thank you Crash, It certainly moves with a lot more purpose than a sphere. I wish I was up there with you.>>

    "Don't worry Control you will be. I'll keep in contact as often as possible to try and stave off going mad from loneliness."

    <<We don't normally go alone.>> the voice of float control added and Crash detected with a note of concern.

"It's okay Control. I know it's unusual, I just needed space for my rescued crew when I get there and although this lady takes four possibly best not to risk more than one on the outward journey." He finished the sentence with a laugh to show he wasn't worried about possible fatalities, but inside he was aware all of this was new to him and he had no real understanding of what troubles he may face. But then neither did anyone else, and that sudden pioneering adventure made him smile and chased away a small shadow that had settled around his soul.

    <<Good luck Crash, call me if you need Me.>> and with that the Harmony went silent and Crash was left with the quiet majesty of space

    ***

Welcome to Jahannam

Of course the flight was long, but it was the most fun Crash had ever had. Harmony's design was an impressive feat of engineering and not without comfort. C.A.K.E had been building spacecraft since the Victorian era and they hadn't lost their eye for interior style. If you were going to be jettisoned into space you wanted a cocoon you were happy to stay confined in for a greater period of time, and although his interior had a slightly more modern look than the crushed velvet of the Spheres it was still better and more stylish than anywhere Crash had ever lived. He took the next part of the journey to set the automatic pilot (he had been informed even at speed he should take time to rest from the controls, as space was in most parts uninspiring and the consol would alert of upcoming issues). With control handed over Crash took the chance to flood the sphere with breathable air, before removing his helmet and the bulkier items needed for launch and all in the wonderful weightlessness of space. Once stripped back to his smart uniform he took to reading the precious dossiers he had been given and wondering what creatures did await him on the mysterious planet.

Chapter 4

The logistics of his journey and how they differed from the spheres was simple; first you had to realise how the spheres worked and the majesty of their design, and second you had to instantly see how that design was flawed when it came to a rescue - at least a rescue with a perceived time limit.

The spheres were, as the name suggests, giant balls very similar in function to a diving bell; a static device that you sat in whilst travelling to your destination with the pull of your craft directing your path. With the diving bell its weight pulled it to the bottom of the sea, a tethered ship could halt that decent and winch you back up, even move you forward but the diving bell itself did very little work. The Spheres were similar in nature; their outsides were covered in cavorite solution, a liquid that blocked gravity in the same way steel blocks light and this meant that no part of them was tethered to anything. When completely shut they appeared to move at lightning speed away from the planet they were once on, the truth however was that they stayed still and the planet continued on its orbit leaving them behind. Once free and in the cold of space the heavenly body you wished to reach would be located and a porthole opened facing it (and only it) The gravitational pull of that body

Welcome to Jahannam

would instantly lock onto the exposed, non cavorite covered surface and the planet, asteroid or star would become the ship upon which you were then tethered. Its movements would become that of the spheres and gravity the winch. The gravitational pull of the object became your speed and the connection remaining unbroken was a factor in safety. For a sphere to reach the planet hidden by the sun it would have to launch, lock onto Mars, Venus or Mercury wait for the hidden planet to appear in their skies and launch again. Sounds simple, but spotting a planet you didn't know existed in the night sky of an alien planet would be a challenge, and landing on an alien planet had its challenges too.

Mercury (for example) was inhabited by a race intelligent enough to have space travel of their own and although they were a race that could be bargained with they were in their way hostile to Earthlings and had been known to visit Earth and abduct our life forms...often showing a preference for female humans or cows. This had obviously caused a problem between the two planets and one that C.A.K.E tried to avoid. Crash had sensibly studied up on the Mercurians before launching , just in case he did have to land and was surprised that although he found the descriptions and pictures of the males of the species quite goblin like he actually found the females more resembling

Earth woman if slightly waif like and strangely winged. Venus too it seemed had a life form and from the crude pictures Crash wasn't sure if it was supposed to be inhabited by squids or pyramids or maybe a strange hybrid of the two. Mars it seemed had many life forms but the more dominant was almost in a perpetual state of warlike hatred of Earth and certainly best avoided.

It was suggested that a sphere could be launched and just wait in space with all ports open, tethered to everything at once like a fly caught in a web. This was of course possible but threw up problems. The first of these problems being the six month wait and that's not to say it wouldn't be longer if the sphere somehow found an orbit of its own around the sun. If it did, then that orbit would certainly be rapidly degrading as the Sun's great gravity pulled them in. But the greater problem was the other planet. The sphere wouldn't be tied to it and winched in at gravitational leisure, which would be the equivalent of trying to catch a moving train by standing in front of it.

So in all honesty Crash was glad that he had the chance to fire up Harmony's engines and actually fly to his destination. His launch into space was exactly as the sphere's would have been, but now he was here Crash was well and truly in control of Harmony's flight path. He was flying away from Earth along her

Welcome to Jahannam

Orbital path. His speed was slightly greater than Earths but in the opposite direction, without the other planet in the way he would meet back up with her in just under six months but as it was he would meet with his destination in just under three; avoid collision by steering wide then entering her atmosphere in the same way the spheres did. Once in the alien planet's sky he could fly Harmony to the beacon and start his rescue. If all went well Lady Belle would have her family back and C.A.K.E (after some additional training) would have a far more efficient way of exploring the cosmos.

"Hello Control, this Is Captain Crash Jackson in the Slingshot "Harmony". I'm just checking in." Crash had been in space a while now, and knew to wait at least two minutes for an answer, it wasn't that anyone wasn't at the helm back in Kent it was just the lag of the radio was complicated, Crash was just glad he could talk to them at all and although casual conversation was brief he was happy to be able to check in daily and know he wasn't alone.

<<We're receiving you Crash>> the friendly female voice of float control finally returned <<Still proceeding with care I trust? Can we have today's data please?>>
Crash reluctantly flipped switches to link Harmony with control so they would get his

flight data fully aware the shared information would slow any conversation to a slower crawl than it already was, but he realised information was more important than chatter at a time like this. Had it truly been just over a month in space? In seemed both an eternity and an instant. As he waited for data to change hands he looked out of his viewing window at the stars. The Earth still showed as a bright light in the darkness, reflecting the Sun's rays so it looked like a tiny star, he thought it would have disappeared by now, obscured by the Sun's position, then he realised the direction he was facing, he scrambled for the radio.

"Control I have clear vision of the planetoid, designation..." Crash paused and looked at his Wallace notes for the official designation number "...127, she just rose out past the Sun. Tell Lady Belle I'll have her family home soon."

Welcome to Jahannam

Chapter 5

Crash circled the planet a couple of times letting the instruments pick up the homing beacon of the missing sphere. From space, this planet certainly had all the hallmarks of Earth. Pale clouds circled in weather patterns whilst great seas washed across her surface defining the continents. The land itself had a more reddish hue than at home and the sea was more akin to a polished mirror, but apart from that he could not help being reminded of the rich green and blue he had left behind.

Finally lights started to flash on the consol and disks spun slowly and with purpose. Crash smiled, comfortable with the knowledge he had pinpointed the location of his rescue mission. He flicked switches and locked in a landing point as best he could with the information he had, but he realised it was going to be more difficult than he had hoped.

The early tests of the ship's skills and manoeuvrability, before he left the pull of Earth, were like skimming and skipping across the atmosphere, gaining speed at best. It hadn't really occurred to Crash that he would have to make a re-entry at that point and now he was wishing he had taken the time to land at least once while he had people to help. Of course the procedure had been discussed thoroughly when he was back in the simulator, but only by people who were basically used to a controlled crash rather than a purposeful landing, and were simply making educated guesses. Angles were discussed in detail and the theory was that if you got it wrong the ship would heat up to such a point the occupants would be cooked inside. Crash had not been happy at this prospect so it was agreed upon that if he didn't feel comfortable flying the Slingshot craft into the planet's atmosphere, then he would have to go old school and let gravity do its thing and land like a sphere. Of course although this method was well documented and easily replicated in the Slingshot craft, the action posed a bigger problem. The spheres were designed to crash - they had buffers, they had armour, they had impact seating; the slingshot had no buffers, no heavy armour and its seat (although the same impact model as the spheres) was not designed to work alone without the other components. That being said, Crash knew he was of no use to the rescue attempt if he was cooked alive. He put on his helmet and gear, and strapped himself into the impact chair as tightly as he could. Then feeling as prepared as he possibly could Crash closed all the cavorite shielding except the anchor spot and like a cannonball he shot downward.

The velocity was certainly the first thing to cope with; Crash hadn't felt speed like this ever. He calculated he must have travelled

Welcome to Jahannam

through space quicker but for some reason the rapid plunge mixed with gravity was tearing at his body, and he could feel both his stomach and consciousness starting to give. The gathering heat wasn't much easier to withstand either. The sphere's armour plating clearly worked as a heat sink, keeping the temperature on the outside. Crash didn't have that luxury, and he was grateful of the circulating air of his helmet that cooled his face at the very least and negated him passing out. For a moment he thought the craft was making a strange noise, it was certainly vibrating enough to, but then the realisation dawned that it was Crash himself making the sound. Issuing a long pained scream through gritted teeth, his fingers dug into the arm rests of his seat.

Then as soon as it all started the sensation stopped. The craft began to cool and the fall was more regular. Reaching his aching fingers forward Crash flipped up all the switches, disengaging the cavorite shields and opening his vision to the alien planet.

The reason for the red hue suddenly became apparent; although still very high above the ground, Crash could see below him miles of undulating red sands, a vast desert of rolling dunes spreading away almost as far as the eye could see, only the reflected glint of the sun off the distant silvery sea was enough to show that the wasteland had ending.

Harmony was in a spin with the air burning around her from the heat of the entry, leaving a smoke trail through the sky. Whichever way the craft turned the landscape didn't change, it simply remained desert. With his head still muggy and his stomach still light and bilious, Crash reached deep inside and found the pilot who had been handed this mission. He brought the control column out from the consol, and with a more hands on feel, started trying to stop the spin. Crash needed engines but the great propellers were unresponsive. The heat of entry had warped the blades enough that they wouldn't turn until cooled. He still had rudder control though, and despite the falling spin he started to rock the ship from side to side. If he was going to come in without power, he wanted to do it as much like a drifting feather as humanly possible and certainly wanted to avoid the thrown brick approach. The repetitive action was working ,the spin was slowing. Crash just had to keep the movements light, simple, not over complicated. It was certainly a bonus that of all the things Captain Jackson knew, he best knew how to crash. Harmony was bending to his will. The spin stopped and although the craft still fell, it was now in a controlled glide. Crash tried the propellers again. Nothing. He needed to show patience, let the wind cool them, let them shrink back to size so they could move in their housing freely again. The desert was getting close and now he could make out details of habitations amongst the dunes; some grand, some humble, many more derelict ruins, already being claimed by the sands. The landscape also changed, sometimes great solid unforgiving outcrops he was glad he was still far above, other times soft moving sand or vegetation trying to find a footing when all around seemed dead and dry.

"Damn it" Crash shouted into his helmet; he was paying too much attention to the desert beyond than he was to the foreground and had not noticed the sudden appearance of a rocky outcrop with an ancient building perched on its edge, until he tore its corner off and something from the underside of Harmony. Then he was again high above the desert. It must have been a temple; people liked to build temples high up where they could see and be seen, but it served as a warning to Crash how close he now was to ditching in the sand. It shot towards him at speed and he gritted his teeth as he carved through the tops of dunes with impressive sprays of red sand. He fired the engines once more, hoping to get height. They spun for a moment, but then he hit a sand dune low enough to not break it apart, and Harmony flipped and came to a jarring rest.

Crash hung upside down in his seat, something

big he had forgotten to tie down before entry
had hit him as Harmony flipped and he could
feel hot, sticky dampness creeping across his
arm. Before him all he could see was red but
then the merciful grip of unconsciousness
slipped into his mind before pain could take
hold.
Blackness.

Welcome to Jahannam

Chapter 6

Scarlett slipped further back into the shadows only stopping when the rough stone of the alcove pressed into her bare flesh, reminding her she had lost her covering tunic for the upcoming deception. The night had already been chill but, here in the darkness of the ruin it lost even the residual heat of the day, until her smooth ebony skin became prickled with tiny bumps .

She reached down and slipped her knife from her long boot; as slowly as possible so as not to make a sound and held her arm loose to her side, keeping the blade behind her legs to avoid any give away flashes of reflected light.

Why was she back in a situation like this again? It seemed like a hundred times she had found herself trapped and in danger and every time it had felt a step closer to her final death. She knew why she did it though. She revelled in the pulse quickening excitement of it all, and tried hard to gain enough composure to still her breath and slow the heart that raced in her chest so fast that it seemed loud enough to give her away. It was certainly that excitement for adventure that had led her here and away from the safety of the Hitherian cities where she had grown up.

Kit Cox

The Hitherians were as close to a peaceful nation as could ever be achieved. They had given up on their warlike history and now led a life of reflective art and hedonistic pursuits. Their bodies had become physical only in the act of pleasure, and their minds had stretched out to sculpt the world around them until they lived in a glorious living canvas. At first, to Scarlett, it had seemed a perfect place to retire from her mercenary life, but soon their lazy disinterest in the world and the skittish fear of the ever present Morn had driven her back into the waste land in search of adventure.

No, this was the life for her, one of adrenalin and adventure. And this current adventure had started mere days ago but already it was coming to its end.

Pursued across the desert with her stolen treasure, Scarlett had tried to shake her foe several times , but to no successful conclusion. She had to make a stand and here on top of an outcrop, one of the many abandoned buildings of the vast wilderness stood waiting. Before her, Scarlett could see the freshly broken rocks of what must have once been a great temple, but was now just a place of shadows in which to hide and spring an ambush. Red weed, from an ancient war, clung to surfaces turning marble to dust and mosaics to scattered bright squares. In the room's centre there stood an ornate but dry fountain with carved beasts and crumbling

Welcome to Jahannam

figures, where Scarlett had discovered a female statue that looked like it was hiding amongst the destructive blood red plant and quickly she formulated a plan. She stripped off her father's distinctive military jacket, leaving herself naked but for her long boots and dressed the statue as a near perfect decoy. The Jacket's material was worn and faded, it had been mended and patched so often it would be unrecognisable to its original owner but to Scarlett it was her father's colours. She still saw it as red as the day she had first wrapped it around her shoulders, its buttons gleaming brightly, and it had become one of the many small treasures she had left from her time with him.

This was a time when her father had taken her away from the comfort of her Mother, and the mocking tones of her people. They had learned to survive in the desert together, a Father and his doting daughter. He taught her how to fight, how to hide, and about his home. He had kept her safe, right up until the day he died. She buried him that same day in the unforgiving sands, never to age further, always to stay the handsome strong soldier.

She of course did not have her father's masculine frame and when she wore his jacket, it hung from her like a thigh length dress, it's sleeves rolled up to expose her delicate hands, the bulk of it pulled in with belts and clever corset like laces. Scarlett may have been a warrior class on a planet of poets but she was still a woman, and would not let eyes pass her over without a flick of recognition or a sparkle of delicious thoughts.

She was not only reliant on the protection of her father's love, held in the uniform she wore; no she also owned a helmet of her Hitherian ancestors. Not the ethereal, artistic brethren of her mother but the beings from whom they had evolved. The Hitherian still kept vast museums of their past, although they visited them infrequently, and it had been as war like and bloody as that of Earth. She had mourned the loss of her father greatly and returned to the city of her birth hoping to be accepted as a servant class like the other Breed children, but had harshly been cast out again. The rejection did her the power of good. Her sorrow turned to strength, and she had returned at night and raided one of the museums and took with her the decorative yet hard wearing tools of her ancestors that she needed to survive in the wilderness. She didn't see it as theft but as a form of ancestor worship that she was sure they would approve of. The helmet was cast from a light yet tough amber metal and had presumably been sculpted to represent a fearsome beast of myth or legend. Its mouth was a finely designed grill that filtered the impurities of the air and its eyes were filled with glass as hard as the metal. One had been designed to look as if it was squinting and it often lead Scarlett to believe no warrior would have worn the helmet into battle as it seriously cut down on vision to the right, meaning you had to survey the land as if you were a predator looking for a feast, constantly turning your head. Thick matted cords gave the headwear the look of hair sprouting from beneath and Scarlett loved the way it would braid with her thick black curls and hold the helmet securely in place as she fought.

She had brought it with her for protection during the upcoming ambush but despite it's worth she chose to let it join her father's jacket on the statue, hiding the marble white face from view and finishing the deception. She briefly regretted that it was not protecting her own head, but its metallic glint would have been a bigger tell than the blade she now twisted in her palm.

A sound came from the doorway and she found herself catching her breath. They had discovered her as expected, and she only had the one chance to make her deception pay.

Her foe, the beasts, walked into the room with a level of wariness more suited to hunted prey than hunter, all eyes on the poorly concealed figure at the fountain. They pressed against the walls either side of the doorway and assessed the situation before them. They had tracked the girl for close on two days and several times she had sought to end their pursuit with rock slides or luring beasts upon them, they had been lucky and were mindfully cautious now they had her cornered in this crumbling temple. She had stolen from them a great prize and not only did they want it back, they also craved to capture her hide for their own needs.

The pursuing creatures were a breed of Morn. Not the bloated Hexaline riders of the desert tribes that Scarlett was used to, but Morn from the low hills and mountain terrains. They bore a more athletic and muscled shape closer to that of the Hitherian, but with their bodies slightly stretched and their legs shorter. Great barrel chests heaved as if they had been running and clouds of steam escaped their lipless mouths as it found the chill air of the temple. Their bodies were covered in a soft red hair but not so dense as to conceal the dark grey skin beneath. Small eyes, jet black and dead to behold scanned the room for high hand holds. The Morn preferred to drop down on their victims and beat them to death with their strong arms and gnarled fists, but Scarlett had chosen her ruin well. What ceiling still remained was too high for even these beasts to leap too and find purchase on.

They were intelligent creatures with their own societies and a hatred of the Hitherian, who had for many years used them as a slave cast before the arrival of the Earthmen and the Breed children. The arrival of the Earthmen and subsequent exodus to the desert had freed them, and now they preyed unmolested on the cities of Jahannam taking the practically defenceless Hitherian inhabitants on a whim, to carry out their sordid desires or more often to be consumed as food.

Scarlett's mother had told her of the tastes of the Morn with such passion that even with her hot human blood the girl had feared them, that was until her Father, with a more reasoned head, had pointed out their weaknesses, to be exploited in times of danger.

These sneaking Morn wore no clothing and so were instantly singled out as the warrior caste of the tribe, by the purposeful and war like scarring that crisscrossed their frames. This meant they could fight and fight well; they were survivors who had earned their place as warriors of their tribe.

Scarlett suddenly felt very naked in their presence, pressed unseen into the alcove but she knew that even naked, she could take down a Morn if given the chance to fight one on one, or even better if she had enough bullets left in her revolver. Of course here she was outnumbered and so guile and cunning had taken sway.

The larger of the two beasts pointed around the walls and she knew they planned to outflank her (well, the statue) and try to take her alive. They were armed with the scavenged weapons of historical invaders, technology greater than their ability to create, but still devastating should they bring the destructive beams to bear. The weapons would leave little but a roasted feast for their bellies and they would get so much more for an intact, living captive so the weapons would be a last resort, even to them. Scarlett's fingers tightened around the handle of her blade as slowly the Morn inched about the room's circumference, eyes not leaving the poorly concealed figure they believed to be their quarry. She could hear the smaller one sniffing the air as it rounded the room. Its flaring nostrils hyper sensitive to her body's natural perfume.

She tried not to sniff the air herself, as the Morn would often smell of fermented milk and sweat, bringing a wave of nausea to even the strongest of stomachs. Then suddenly it was before her alcove, not much taller than her, but its naked back a knot of tensing muscles, its buttocks strong and pert. Without hesitation she leapt from the shadows like a blast of furnace air, landing on the Morn's back and thrusting the blade deep into its neck with skilful accuracy, she felt the strong muscles of the neck part beneath the metal and heard the soft pop of the skin as it gave to the tempered point. The creature barely let out a sound as the razor sharp blade severed the windpipe. Its short legs

Welcome to Jahannam

buckled as life left its body, but she instinctively wrapped her free arm about its throat taking the weight of the creature and halting its fall. The bestial reek was strong, as two days of hunting her had put it under excursions most Morn would not look to undergo in a month. It was heavy too and she stumbled forward into the greater light shining in from the hole in the damaged roof. It was this movement that actually gave her actions away to the larger hunter. She deftly whipped her blade from the gushing neck, the blood acting as a lubricant and hurled it at the second creature, sending the weapon spinning like a wheel across the temple. Her luck was out, as it failed to embed in her victim's forehead and instead only took the creature's ear and scored a gash across its shoulder. She let out a frustrated cry as she had been aiming to split its face in two.

Although not a killing blow the Morn let forth a howl of pain, its hand going to its damaged head, giving Scarlett a satisfactory buzz of excitement and allowing her precious seconds to seize an advantage. She swing her tightly held victim's heat ray upwards and with a purposeful and practiced flick of switches, incinerate the Morn across from her where he stood.

The slung weapons of the Morn were far less devastating devices than they would have been when new and in the grip of the cephalopod invaders from which they were scavenged, and so instead of a stone melting heat they caused a moderately satisfying burn. So rather than a cloud of ash, the charred but still distinguishable shape of her enemy fell onto the ornate floor of the Temple, dead but far from cold.

Victorious, she dropped her Morn corpse shield, allowing it to spill its blood across the tiles and fill the air with its strange sweetness. The smells of the beast's exterior were not matched by its interior, which had a surprisingly pleasing smell and taste. Scarlett licked the blood from her hand as she walked across the ruin to retrieve her knife.

Two days of chase for mere seconds of heartless slaughter, but it had certainly been a case of them or her and she certainly had enjoyed every second of the fight, almost as much as she had enjoyed the last two days of pursuit. She picked up the blade and toasted it clean on the body of the charred, still burning Morn, before returning it to its sheath.

A rumble in the night sky predicted the chance of a storm and as she looked up she cursed the temples lack of a decent roof.

Welcome to Jahannam

Chapter 7

The morning found Scarlett stiff from an uncomfortable night's sleep, wedged in the driest space the temple had available to her; cut off from escape by the breaking storm. This was not a problem everywhere, but the rain in the desert had been known to come down so hard that it could sap you instantly of strength and draw blood; enough rain in the desert and you could die. If you grew up in the desert the chance of walking in the rain lost any thought of romance and a sensible adventurer would find close shelter and wait it out.

She awoke and took time to stretch; rubbing feeling back into her limbs as she checked the area was safe, before walking cautiously out into the temple's main room. Scarlett looked around and was surprised to find one of the Morn missing. Often scavengers would take what carrion they could from a fight, but they were not quiet creatures and she was glad whatever had the strength to drag a dead Morn away into the night had not found her asleep and unaware of its presence. For a moment her mind drifted to her prize, but she knew it was well bound and sealed away from the questing noses of Jahannam's finest predators.

The cooked Morn was also moved some distance from its previous spot, backing up the theory that something had tried to clear the room of energy giving food, rather than the more unappealing thought that her blade hadn't gone quite deep enough the night before to still her foe forever and they had somehow found strength to crawl away.

Scarlett gathered up the bowls she had used to collect the night's rain water and carefully tipped the precious liquid into her canteens until all were full, then she satisfied her morning thirst with what was left.

Her eyes were drawn to a section of the roof that was festooned with red weed, and the water that still ran heavily from the hanging tendrils draining off some unseen reservoir of rain from the storm. She passed her hand beneath the expelling water and was pleased to find it had already been heated by the fierce morning sun. Not wishing to miss the free shower she slipped off her boots and stepped beneath the falling water. The wonderfully warm cascade instantly began to wash weeks of trail dust, blood and sweat from her body until she glistened in reflected light.

Her hair became darker as the water saturated it, and as the dusty afro became heavier it hung down in long ringlets clinging to the curves of her body. Then, as weeks of neglect where washed free from every strand, it seemed to glow with the same radiance attributed to the high born Hitherian women.

Welcome to Jahannam

Her body, now washed free of grime, became rich ebony in direct contrast to the alabaster statues that gazed on with sightless eyes, silently watching as her shapely limbs ran with droplets of fresh warm water dampening the soft curls between her thighs. She tipped her head up into the torrent and parted her full lips letting her mouth fill with the warm tide, before swishing and spouting the liquid playfully out onto the wall before her, like a jet.

Scarlett watched the weed and grime break from the walls surface, beneath which wonderful colours shone through prompting her to brush her hand across the ingrained filth and fill her mouth with another cleaning blast.

Slowly revealed before her was a wonderfully artistic mural, of Hitherian priests and acolytes pouring offerings of gold into a fountain, celebrating some long forgotten religious pomp and ceremony. Scarlett turned to face the room's central decoration, which had aided as her distraction the night before. It was unmistakably the fountain from the picture; although encrusted with weed and grime of many untended years.

Intrigued, Scarlett walked dripping from the natural shower, leaving perfectly shaped, wet footprints on the ruined mosaic floor as she moved towards the ornament at the room's heart. In two bounds she had climbed to its top. She was then so still that to any casual eye entering the room now, she would have appeared just as any other carving within the temple with perfect dusky curves, entwined amongst the pure white marble and flowing vibrant vines.

Her climb and stillness were rewarded as her eyes adjusted to the gloom and revealed the fountains pinnacle was indeed a vast tube leading down beneath the temple and from the hot sun shining through the ruined roof she could see many objects glinting far below.

It was true that being a breed made her a second class citizen, but to the Hitherian even a breed with money was elevated higher than their station and given the respect she craved. She had at first tried to gain social elevation by heroically protecting her people from Morn raids, but when that had proved fruitless she chose instead to make money from the same action but as a mercenary service. It turned out to be a slow and dangerous process and she suspected she would die long before she bought respect; however treasure hunting (or theft) of an abandoned temple was a far simpler means of gaining cash and this looked like quite a haul.

Turning onto her back, Scarlett slid down over the statue, through the weed to the temple floor and crossed quickly to her clothes. She had planned to move on, but it seemed an investigation was now in order.

Welcome to Jahannam

It felt like the first time she'd been properly dressed in many hours. Her Fathers jacket had washed through in the rain and was still damp, which was a relief as it seemed like a waste to get so clean only to dress back in the same filth soaked garments she'd been wearing for days. After it's soaking, it was clear to see the jacket was red and immensely practical as camouflage against the sand and weed. It finished half way down her thigh so didn't hamper movement in any way and was thick natural fibre giving some protection without being hot under the sun. A heavy leather belt around the waist and various straps and lacing held it in tightly and accentuated her curves. Her legs were long and smooth but became protected as she pulled back on the knee length boots; which in turn were also a hand me down from her father. These too were patched and mended, but she had an array of trinkets sewn to the tops and entwined with the laces to make them more feminine, without removing their practicality.

She then slung across one shoulder the strap of the Morn's heat ray, and on the other she slid a British issue rifle (unfortunately not her father's and currently out of bullets.) At her hip was a holstered revolver and placed back in the boot, the deadly knife.

Thus attired she walked out to her vehicle, concealed beneath a cover that made it look like just another part of the scenery and uncovered just the trunk and removed a thin but strong rope from within.

Lying behind the vehicle was the makeshift travois she had been towing as she drove, more like a trailer than a stretcher. She had cursed how much it had slowed her at times allowing the Morn to get so close but she was sure the stolen cargo was worth it.

Scarlett would happily scavenge to find goods to trade. She would sometimes steal from the human cities but more often than not she would hunt and bring back meat, or trinkets from ruins. The object she had towed had fallen from the sky like a bright comet and she had noted it's decent as something to be investigated the next day. She, however, was beaten to her quarry by a Morn hunting party and found she had to watch helpless from the dunes as they pulled what was clearly a human from the wreckage of his strange craft. Morn preferred their meat fresh as opposed to dried so had acquired an ingenious method of preserving freshness. The lands of the Morn were littered with carnivorous plant life and many preserved the bodies of their victims to a horrific half life as they were devoured. Before a raid the Morn would simply dig up several of these plants and remove the digestion sacs. Any animal caught could be placed in the giant leaves which would contract naturally and keep

Welcome to Jahannam

the cargo fresh and alive yet sedated in a dreamless sleep until the Morn returned home and released their food to the grateful kitchens. Human flesh, she was informed, was not as sweet as Hitherian but it was rare so would fetch a good price.

Of course Scarlett had no desire to eat the Human, she was clearly after any bounty she could get on saving a life or the life debt she would be owed, which were often worth more than rewards and could be called on for far longer than the debt really warranted. Of course for most of this, the cargo needed to be alive.

She had no idea if the Human was dead but right now she was more than happy to leave the pleasingly shaped pod on its stretcher for a future investigation while she went back into the temple and gathered it's treasures, knowing that the suspended nature of the sleep also had healing properties and she'd rather her rescued human was in fine form than close to death and needing care. Also if she was going to give a first impression, she wanted it to be well thought out not a blurted giggly mess. Besides, she liked her own company and wasn't good at sharing.

Feeling happy and refreshed she was now prepared for a descent into a dark hole in the ancient temple, and she headed back inside the ruins. In the day light it was easy to see the Temple sat high up on a cliff top and whatever was beneath it was clearly descending down inside the cliff so it was less about descending into the bowels of the planet and more about heading for a lower level.

She removed her helmet from the statue that had served as a distraction the night before, and put it on. Once again the statue came in handy as she tied her rope around it several times, ensuring a good tight bond before throwing the other end into the hole at the fountain top.

The climb was fairly easy as the rope simply descended down unhindered. Scarlett found herself gracefully wrapping coils about her arm and sliding into the dark, her boots touching the surface of glittering goodies that moved about beneath her, but presumably from years of rusting had become a more solid lump so on the whole was fairly stable. The night's rain had clearly got in too, as the pile was wet and slippery. Scarlett made sure she crouched and steadied herself with her hands as well as her feet before making any greater moves. She didn't like to wear the helmet when she was in a space she did not know, as it cut down on many of her senses but she had seen more creatures die from head injuries than she had witnessed die from poor vision or restricted hearing. She waited for a while until her natural senses had warmed to the gloom before reaching up to the helmet's peak and sliding a

Welcome to Jahannam

switch. The simple action initiated a mechanism inside, that lowered a mineral stick into a tube of clear liquid and by some arcane chemical reaction she had a beam of light shining from a grill on her forehead. She had chosen well when liberating this cleverly designed helmet from the museum. The chamber, now better lit, turned out to be little more than an oubliette, but Scarlett knew at once she was not alone. Something else was in the darkness. She could hear it and now she thought about it, there was most certainly a smell, two smells in fact; there was the sweet smell of Morn blood and a darker underlying smell of ...fish?

It couldn't be, most of the waterways of the desert had been evaporated and only the greatest Hitherian cities still lay on carefully channelled rivers, which was why they remained mainly unmolested by Humans. Even the Morn had lost most of their frozen stores of water over the years and it was only because Scarlett had travelled further afield that she even knew the smell of fish (well the aquatic kind, most knew the fresher smell of the air kind as they were a strong trade item and swam happily in the skies over most of Jahannam).

Cautiously Scarlett swung her beam of light down onto the ground. The floor was thick with dry mud that was flaking up in scale-like patterns from heavy flagstones. Many things sparkled under the light, not fish but gems and amongst them were the tarnished trinkets and dulled metal of ancient coins. It dawned on her that this had once been a tank, full of water and topped by a fountain. The people above must have thrown in good luck coins and treasures in exchange for wishes (although they possibly called them prayers). The priests had made greater offerings, possibly on high holy days, as Jahannam was once peppered with religions to all kinds of natural phenomena, however, she knew at once this was not people worshiping an empty tank of water. They had found some kind of beast to rise up to the status of deity. Its tank had dried as the religion had died but that's the thing with creatures that live in desert water, so many have a knack for surviving the droughts, only to come to life and feed at the first sign of rain and last night that storm had been fierce. Scarlett was pretty sure the Morn hadn't crept down here himself, and for something to be worshipped as a God on Jahannam it normally had to be quite impressive in size. Moving slowly she wrapped her arm back into the rope' She was unsure if this had been the wrong move or if the strike was just coincidence but out of the gloom something hard and long flew. It hit her like a Morn fist, and had she been on safer ground she would have rolled with the impact. Here though, the platform beneath her feet tipped as she leant. Its slick recently wet surface was no place to find purchase. Her legs

Welcome to Jahannam

went from beneath her and she would have slipped harmlessly down the side of the fused treasures, possibly to a place she could gain her thoughts, but her recently entwined arm brought her up short and the wrench on her shoulder at the sudden stop sent a wave of pure pain through her upper body and a yelp escaped her lips as the arm dislocated from its socket. She let the rope un-twine and lowered herself painfully down to the cracked mud floor hoping whatever struck her was the other side of the heap of offerings.

She didn't have the time for a dislocated limb so she surged forward onto the pile of treasure and felt her arm pop back into its socket; the action brought fresh pain but this time she bit back the yelp. The pile before her rocked alarmingly as something heavy moved up its far side, and soon the creature of the temple was sat above her on its hoard.

It was a toad of monstrous proportions, its wart encrusted skin cracked from many years without water, its belly distended from the recent meal of the Morn - a meal that disturbingly still hung from its mouth in the form of a gnarled grey hand. It opened its gullet and the last of its meal slid out of sight revealing that within its mouth laid not one purple tongue but several, all as thick as a strong mans arm. The creature stretched its limbs out as if trying to find a better grip on the unstable platform it now stood upon. However its limbs kept slipping and stretching to their full length, revealing that either from illness or a previous struggle it had lost the greater part of one of its back legs. It seemed to inflate itself slightly and puffed out small clouds of discoloured smoke. Scarlett was aware of the creatures, of course there were smaller versions all over the desert if you knew where to look and were hungry enough, but this one had grown to titanic proportions compared to its more common brethren. Her Father had made it his earliest lesson to get his daughter to know all the flora and fauna he thought she would meet on her travels, and although she had listened to the stories she somehow hadn't expected to be coming across one of the Jahannam toads that had grown quite so large. The smoke was a paralysing cloud of gas used to stun its prey, but she knew well that even this big the toad needed to be a lot wetter for the poison sacks to produce it in any threatening levels to her. She also knew not to take the risk of assumption so stooping slowly she picked up a large gold platter from the floor. It scraped alarmingly and the dehydrated amphibian rolled its eyes in her direction. Quick as a flash one of its many tongues shot out and Scarlett instinctively raised the heavy platter up like a shield, deflecting the sticky appendage. She rolled across the floor as another tongue struck where she had once stood, sending clouds of silt dust and precious stones into the air. She continued the roll and another couple of strikes filled the air with yet more detritus before she sprang to her feet and sent the platter spinning towards the open gullet like a discus. The platter found new deadly purpose as a discus and severed a tongue off at its base before it embedded in the soft tissue of the throat, sealing the glands that expelled the poisonous gas. It had not been Scarlett's plan but it was certainly fortuitous. The toad recoiled from the impact but kept its footing on top of the heap, before starting to use a front leg to try and dislodge the disk that was now firmly jammed in its mouth.

Scarlett took the chance to un-holster her revolver and take up a good stance. She tried her hardest not to fire the handgun too often, as bullets were hard to come by and expensive to have made, but she now had the heat ray and would trade that in for more ammunition for her precious gun. She aimed at the large red eye that rolled uncomfortably as the creature played at the protrusion stuck fast in its mouth, and pulled the trigger. In the enclosed space the guns retort was instantly deafening and the flash from the barrel robbed her of sight. She cursed her own foolishness shaking her head as she stumbled about stunned, ears ringing, dots before her closed eyes. The strange design of the helmet had possibly saved her sight but its metal design had not dulled the sound of the blast, so it was her vision that recovered first, allowing her a look towards her target. The giant toad lay slumped on the huge pile of rusted wealth, its ruined eye dripping a sickly ooze down its rough skinned cheek and the socket burning with a dull orange flame as the dry creature reacted to the heat of the projectile. At first she thought it still breathed as its throat sack continued to expand, but then realised it just continued to fill with the trapped poisonous gas. Too late the possibility occurred to her of the gas being flammable, and a small trickle of smoke escaped from beneath the wedged disk curling up to the hot flame that crackled around the eye socket. As if the touch paper had been lit, the deity exploded.

If the gun had been a mistake the sudden explosion had been more so. The vast heap of treasure beneath the beast remembered it had once been a mass of individual items and they left the stack with purpose. Flying in all directions with such force large platters embedded in walls and heavy broaches shattered brickwork.

Scarlett was caught in the blast and was thrown to the floor as something slammed hard into her side cutting through her father's coat and slicing through her soft flesh. The pain was unbearable as it blossomed out through her

Welcome to Jahannam

body and she was robbed of her senses by the cold embrace of unconsciousness.

Chapter 8

The muzziness was the first thing to return, creeping stealthily into her head like the unwanted morning that inevitably followed a night of celebration. The pain was not so subtle in its attack. Her side felt numb at first until she moved, and then it came like hot fingers reaching in to play her nerves like a harp. She was not one for the advertising of personal pain and weakness but her mouth opened in a scream as sharp as the debris lodged in her side.

Her fingers found the warm sticky mess that her eyes could not yet focus to see and she felt her stomach turn. Her helmet had come free in the blast and its light shone away from her, illuminating the damage upon the wall and the sparkle of the red dust in the air. She had no way of pulling herself from the pit - that was obvious. The rope now hung a small distance from the floor and could have been reached with an easy leap if she was in peak condition but as it transpired she was injured badly and trapped.

A grim reality passed into her mind. She was certainly not without food as bits of the toad god littered the floor, some of them helpfully cooked. With luck and rest she could last a week or two on the puddles of water and scattered meat. Maybe even recover enough strength to try for the rope. She was aware from

Welcome to Jahannam

bruises on her body she had already been down the pit for hours lying motionless on the hard floor. If she was going to die from bleeding out, it would have happened already. Infection was going to be her problem now. Her father's coat had a soft lining she had often prized, as it felt good against her skin, but now it could be her saviour too. She pulled herself over to her fallen knife, holding back the pain that wanted to escape her lips and started to cut a wide bandage from the fabric. She was careful to cut in a way that the soft lining could be washed and replaced at a later time if she escaped.

She had one flask of fresh water and using it sparingly cleaned the wound. Small coloured gems glittered within her flesh but she chose not to remove them and start her bleeding again, but instead bound herself tight. After a time she was finished and sat on the floor, wound bound, easing the uniform jacket back on to keep her body from shivering in the dark. She picked up and chewed on a slab of the creature. It tasted like putrid fish and oozed grease and oil that ran unappetisingly down her throat. She was hardened to the poisons of creatures and plants but detected none of the bitter, acrid tastes in the flesh so deduced she could eat her fill rather than just enough to avoid death.

Her meal she washed down with a mix of the pure water and some gathered from a puddle but it sat heavy in her stomach and made her want to stand and move to quell the uncomfortable feeling. She however realised the more important value of rest so instead dragged herself over to what was left of the treasure pile, and propped up as comfortable as possible she fell into a deep sleep.

Her rest was dreamless in the main; a body used to the hazards of the world has a memory for knitting itself back together when given the proper respect, but it is an ability that borrows heavily from the other senses. So when dreams started to surface they were abstract and full of lessons.

The vast toad creature was hidden in shadows and its pile of treasure was now a charnel heap of bones and the detritus of the dead. Scarlett dangled like a small desert spider on its thread as she lowered into the open mouth of the creature; a dark purple cave that dripped with clear glistening grease and grew darker until the myriad of gems embedded in the flesh shone out like stars.

The touch of the hand in the darkness made her recoil, and instincts honed by years of hunting snapped her from her dreams . The hand that actually caressed her face she grabbed, and her knees went instinctively up to cover her body with the hard natural shield of her shins. The pain returned as her body curled at the waist and she let out a cry that brought

Welcome to Jahannam

tears to her eyes and unfurled her like a flower, her back arching with the agony of it, so close to pleasure yet so far removed. She rolled on her side and clasped both hands to her wound feeling the heat of fresh blood soaking her dressing.

"Be still." It was a deep male voice and it came from the shadows before her. The Morn had voices and words but they would not waste any on a Hitherian so she knew at least the risk was not as great. She opened her eyes and turned to face the figure that waited just outside the beam of the well's light. "If I approach again you must remain still, I wish you know harm."

Scarlett couldn't believe it, the words were English like her father's so she simply nodded and the figure came into view. She knew at once he was a human for his face had the dark shadow that foretold of the beginnings of a beard and his hair was a chestnut brown.

"Seems we've both woken up feeling a bit out of sorts old Gal." He said seemingly to himself as he looked over the prostrate form before him, not really sure if she spoke his language at all but very aware she was wearing what appeared to be a vintage British infantry uniform.

Scarlett in turn looked over the human and she knew at once this was her "package", somehow awake. Although she had only seen

90

him at a distance, before his freshness wrapping had been applied he had a distinctive look and apparel . He was taller than her, but then most humans were. A much prized attribute if you went by the gossip of the Hitherian women, who would giggle along with their stories of the great size and strength of the warriors of Earth. It was this that had lead to so many Breed being born. You'd be easily forgiven to think they were Giants if you listened to the gossip and it was only because she had often passed into their cities that she knew there was certainly not that much difference in their size from Hitherian males.

The darkness of the beard was something she had missed, as it was a trait missing on Hitherian men including her breed brothers. Even the Morns who were far hairier than her kinfolk had faces devoid of growth. As he bent down she instinctively reached up to touch and was reminded at how hard and prickly the hair was. The touch prompted him to look deep into her eyes as if questioning her actions. She pulled her hand away quickly

"Hello." She said through the pain lacing her muscles.

The man's face became quizzical and his brow rose for a second before hardening up "Well that certainly answers that question." He sat on the pile beside her as the strength went from his legs and he realised he needed a sit down.

***

Crash could just about remember the ditching of Harmony in the sand dunes, and he had a strange feeling monkey men had removed him from his seat, but beyond that he remembered little. He must have dreamed of dying because waking up encased in leathery petals had been a surprise. He had forced himself free to discover that the alien pod was lashed to a makeshift stretcher like the Indians used, tied behind the strangest of vehicles made from bits of plane and what looked like train parts, hidden beneath a camouflaged cover. The absent driver clearly must have been trying to help, so he went in search of them.

Entering the temple he glanced up through the ruined roof and suddenly realised this was the building he had hit during entry. A quick search of the fresh rubble and he found the part he had heard torn off by the impact, he slipped it into his pocket in case it turned out to be important. The sky outside was cloudless but there was a feel in the air that suggested there had been a recent, much needed storm. He kicked something and glanced down from the heavens to be met with the charred remains of what was certainly once a man or possibly one of the monkey creatures he believed had pulled him from Harmony. It seemed to Crash he may be far from home, but he was never far from war or violence. There was an oozing to the body and he was aware something had been eating it, the realisation causing him to cast his eyes suspiciously about the temple that he now found himself in. Small things scuttled fast in the shadows, stopping to watch what they may have believed was a larger scavenger.

He was feeling somewhat out of his depth, either his rescuers had met their demise in this ruin or they had caused the death of the poor fella on the floor, bringing up the worry their intentions may not have been as pure as he first hoped. The tied rope on the ornate fountain drew his attention and he found himself scaling the entwined statues to follow where it went.

The pit was certainly dark and had a distinct reek of the sea about it. In the pit's gloom far below him laid a girl the tied rope ending some way above her head. He tried to hail her but she didn't move. From this distance she could be dead, but he couldn't take that risk. She certainly wasn't the daughter he was looking for but she appeared human. He loosened the rope a bit so it reached the floor and shinned down. The movement as he put his feet on the ground seemed to stir her, but it could easily have been caused by the unstable pile on which she lent, so he reached out and touched her face to check for warmth. That's when she had woken and ended up bleeding and in pain.

***

Scarlett shifted to reveal the blood soaked bandage and was strangely comforted by the Earthman's sharp intake of breath as he showed empathy at her wound.

"I think I need to have a better look at it. Are you okay for me to remove the bandage?" he said compassionately. Scarlett nodded her approval. She had patched herself up, but was fully aware that other eyes and hands would be an advantage.

The Earthman removed his heavy gloves and started to unwind the bandage, before leaning in for a better look. He glanced about and grabbed the helmet and after a brief look at it, shone the head torch clearly onto the wound.

"You've got something embedded in there. We're going to have to take it out if you want to heal!" He said, not looking up from his examination.

Scarlett had wanted to leave the object in, she had no idea of what it could be holding together and she certainly didn't want more pain. "I'd rather it.." She let out a cry of pain as her standby medic pulled the foreign body quickly from her wound. There was an instant relief from the discomfort and numbness flooded her side. "..What the Hell?" She shouted, and smacked the man around the arm.

94

Crash laughed and let drop from his hand a blood stained locket, so it dangled from his fingers by its chain. Then bending forward he placed it over her head so it adorned her neck "Don't worry I'm not stealing it." He quipped and went back to the wound. "Its sealing quite nicely by itself now that's gone, you'll get a scar but if you allow me to stitch it up it will be quite a delicate one."

"Well you can't cause me much more pain than you just did, so feel free." She said bravely, lifting the locket from her chest to examine its delicate carved surface.

"What's your name?" Asked the man, as he took what looked like a tobacco tin from his pocket and opened it to reveal, plasters, thread, needles and other helpful but small items.

"It's Scarlett." She answered quickly, before adding "Scarlett Byrne." Hoping the man, who spoke English like her father, might show some recognition of the name but instead he just laughed.

"It's a perfectly good name." she said defensively as he threaded a curved needle.

"Oh I agree, it's lovely. It's just folks all call me Crash and I was amused that together we are Crash and Burn." He chuckled again and this time Scarlett joined in. That was until he slipped the needle through her flesh.

Welcome to Jahannam

Chapter 9

It was a little later, when hand over gloved hand, Crash started to pull the two of them back up the rope and out of the fountain. Scarlett was on Crash's back, her arms around his neck her legs wrapped around his waist. The helmet was strapped to her back like a bucket, and was full of the most expensive and unique looking of the trinkets and gems, while the guns were slung over Crash's shoulder.

As they climbed she couldn't help but appreciate the smell of him. The leaves in which he had been wrapped had given his skin a bark like smell and beneath this his skin smelt warm , with the musk of a man that had not yet turned stale. It had been a long time since she'd been this close to an Earthman and a happy sigh escaped her lips.

"You okay?" Crash asked pausing on the climb, thinking the strain must be pulling on the freshly stitched wound.

"Yeah, Yeah! I'm fine." She blustered almost cursing herself for the slip.

"Just wrap your leg's tighter around me and let me do the work." He said helpfully, not seeing Scarlett bite her bottom lip and close her eyes as she complied with his request.

Soon they broke out from the shadow of the fountain and back into the uncomfortable heat of the temple, and Scarlet quickly got off of the pilots back and adjusted her tunic.

Crash turned and looked at the woman in the light for the first time. She was dressed in clothes he could only describe as hand downs from the glory days of the British Empire. He was pretty sure the adapted red dress was once a British army tunic and the knee high boots were also vintage military issue, add to that personal adaption and you were close. The woman wearing them was gorgeous; her skin was dark like the West Indian soldiers he had fought alongside and her hair was jet black and full, framing her head like a soft helmet of curls.

"I need you to take me back to my spaceship." It was an abrupt way of asking but Crash couldn't think of any other way and he hoped to God Scarlett knew where it was. Scarlett placed her hand on the bandaged and stitched wound before answering, feeling it beneath her fingers. It threw her hips to the side and gave her a stance that looked as if he had asked for far too much than he was entitled.

"Fine, I can take you back but I don't know how much use your spaceship will be; it fell from the sky on fire."

***

Crash looked around the interior of the propeller car, the worn leather seats, the detritus of a life lived in a confined space, blankets and

Welcome to Jahannam

cushions pushed aside with dirty clothes hidden beneath, the tell tale signs of a person's private life laid bare.

The car's body was a plane's fuselage, it lacked wings but It had four large train wheels cleverly mounted on the sides, its tail section was opened up to allow more space inside (no need to keep it light) and the whole thing was sealed shut from the elements and finished off with many adapted parts of a carriage including roof, doors and lights. It looked amazing as if it had always been built this way but most importantly it still had the planes large wooden propeller that spun out front courtesy of the well kept engine; the only change to its set up being that the blades of the propeller were now protected from the desert's flipped up stones by a circular metal cage. The whole thing was painted as close to British racing green as you could get, and the exterior shone with the love of a good pilot and mechanic.

Scarlett still had the two Vickers machine guns mounted either side and (Crash guessed) cleverly set up to the timing of the propeller. All in all it was a genius adaption and Crash felt very comfortable inside.

"Where did you get all this?" Crash finally asked from the back seat having had a good look around.

Scarlett glanced around her at the cockpit, as if seeing the car for the first time before answering "Stuff just kind of comes with the storms. You watch the skies, you wait till the Menhune move away any bigger problems, then you swoop in and hope to get something good before anyone else does." She turned and smiled at Crash "I kind of figured you blew in with a storm."

He couldn't help but laugh as she clearly added humour to the last comment. "I didn't, but I did come here to find someone that did. That's why I need to get back to Harmony, she has the device that tells me where they are." "Harmony?" Scarlett asked with suspicion but also with a moment of dread; she had watched the Morn pull only one person from the crash and they didn't leave meat behind unless it was very spoiled.

"It's the name of the ship." Crash answered not picking up on any tone, but instead looking from the windows to watch the desert go past. It was starting to sink in that he was on an alien planet; this train of thought however lead to another question. "You speak English?" "My father was an Earthman, he taught me his language; saved him from learning my mother's tongue I guess. But I'm not from Earth. I'm a Breed." she said hoping it would explain everything and finish the line of questioning.

Welcome to Jahannam

"A breed of what?" Crash asked cautiously.

"Not of what, just a Breed. Neither Hitherian nor Human." She added slowly as if talking to a child.

"Ahh! So from mixed parentage, that's cool. I suddenly thought your head was going to split in half and tentacles were going to come out." He laughed somewhat nervously, aware that might still happen.

"You're not shocked? You're not going to shun me?" she questioned sceptically, fully aware from both her Hitherian dealings and her Father that being Breed was a thing to be ashamed of; something you kept to yourself, especially around other humans.

Crash looked at the back of her head, aware she hadn't looked at him once through the exchange "Why would I be shocked? I'm sure your mother and father loved each other very much, it just sounds a bit racist."

"All of my kind are called Breed, to the Hitherian we are the new worker class, especially since the Morn left the high born." She said unsurely, as if a big bit of her life was about to tumble away. There was an awkward pause before she continued "Did I look like tentacles would come out of my head then?"

Crash laughed again. "Not really, it was just I was reading a dossier on my journey and there's a planet called Uranus where a fungoid predator can take the form of anything it likes, to attract and fool its prey and when it turns back it normally starts with tentacles." The last comment felt rude as he was technically the alien race here so he changed the subject. "So how long have Earthmen been coming to ...what do you call this planet by the way?" "Depends on who you talk to, the Hitharians call it Hither but everyone else, including the Morn, call it Jahannam. As for how long Earthmen have been coming here, well I guess for most of written history." She turned and looked at her passenger "Do they not talk of us on Earth?"

Crash looked guilty "Not really, the whole going to other planets thing has been kept hushed up. The people I came here for had no idea anyone else had even visited Jahannam before. I think they thought the storms that took the people I'm here to rescue were a one off, although research suggested differently. From what you say however Earthmen have been coming for a while, certainly if there's enough cross breeding to contribute a new racial class."

Scarlett coughed derisively "Wow! You really don't know our history do you. The storms bring warriors from your planet to ours." She tapped the dashboard of the propeller car fondly "And whatever might be around them at the time. The Hitherian stayed in the desert

Welcome to Jahannam

though, and managed to avoid most of them - their monsters, wars and growing cities. We weren't lucky enough to avoid the cephalopods when they chose to invade though. The Cephalopods simply came to conquer, and enslaved the Hitherian whilst doing it - used them for food and grew the horrible red weeds you see everywhere until they choked the precious waterways with it and killed the desert. Seems they had a thing for the heat and no home of their own, so they took my ancestors home instead and made it theirs. The Hitherian had turned from their warrior ways eons before and lived a hedonistic life of peace and art; they were an easy target. It must have all seemed lost.

Then the Earth armies came in their droves, great armies of red coated soldiers in flying ships, with powerful guns. They fought the Cephalopods without fear, drove them back and destroyed their factories and war machines; freed the Hitherian from slavery into the bargain. Freed the Morn too. There had apparently been a prophesy that Earth was next, so they found out where the Cephalopods were camped up and took the fight to them. They didn't come by storm though, they opened windows of their own and just flew through. Of course they stayed afterwards to make sure the threat was gone and that's when the Breed started to appear."Scarlett sucked her teeth "Soldiers on leave."

The car went quiet for awhile as Scarlett was left with her thoughts and Crash let his mind run through the many stories of his mother's. He could recall at least several that would have tied in with this whole battle with the Cephalopods but he was sure she had always said Mars, the red planet. She even had added the detail of the red sand being everywhere when they got back. Suddenly his eyes were on the great red desert beyond the windows, and his mother's stories didn't seem so fantastical.

"I've heard these tales before. That was forty, fifty years ago, surely?" Crash added prompting Scarlett to look back at him for a second."

"So you have heard of us before. Yes the Cephalopod war was possibly fifty years ago now, my Father was wounded as a young bombardier and chose to stay behind, said he felt more accepted here. Jahannam has a strange effect on the entropy of Earth born; you don't really age here or succumb to disease or infection. If anything you grow stronger. I think he felt that to stay he had a chance of a life, then he met my mother and they had me. The Hitherian weren't prepared to treat his daughter as an equal so he took me out into the desert and taught me how to survive, how to make do and mend. My mother just let me go."

Welcome to Jahannam

Crash didn't need to ask of her father, he could tell from the way her words seemed filled with sorrow and the clothes she wore that the old soldier from Earth was no longer with them, and he didn't want to bring further sorrow by enquiring why. He had seen a lot of families torn apart by war, and despite all advice he found it very helpful to bottle up the pain.

"Did you never seek out the other Earthmen?" He asked after thoughtful reflection.

"I did, but they saw me as much as an outsider as the Hitherian. Humans trust little that comes from the deserts on Jahannam. We're too close to the Persians and all their perversions."

"Persians from Earth?" Crash interrupted.

"Yes Persians from Earth, legend says they were the first that the storms brought; some kind of ancient punishment that just kept preying on the warlike and seeking out the Titans they created."

Crash leant forward on the back of her seat suddenly more interested in the conversation. "The Titans.... The giant creatures? That's who the storms are for?" he blurted.

Scarlett looked him square in the face her features amused "Who knows, it was centuries ago. As I said, legend says. It does tie in nicely but then legend always does, and it's easy to make legends up about people who barely ever leave their walled cities. The Titans come and the Menhune clear them away. The warriors

come and they start disorientated and confused,
but then wander off out of the desert and start
settlements of their own. It's the great big circle
of life."

Crash was about to ask about the Menhune
when Scarlett stopped the propeller and they
slid to a halt in the sand. "We're here. Seems
we were closer than I thought, must have taken
a few weird turns trying to shake off your
captors."

Scarlett pointed to the dunes and Crash
could just make out the half buried and
upturned shape of Harmony through the settling
cloud of sand

.

Welcome to Jahannam

Chapter 10

Harmony was easier to right than Crash had thought, and the sand had clearly cushioned rather than crushed the shell on impact. Soon they were both inside, and Scarlett was much taken by the interior. She lay sprawled on the bed stretching out like a contented cat.

"This bed is amazing. "She almost purred. Crash was trying not to be distracted and used his time to recalibrate the beacon and set the radio.

"Control. This is Captain Jackson of the slingshot craft Harmony. I have landed...safely and made contact with the locals." He looked across at Scarlett her back arched, eyes closed in an unkempt state of bliss. "They appear friendly."

He fiddled with the beacon whilst waiting for a reply, aware Scarlett was now on her side watching him.

<<Welcome back Crash. We lost contact for a bit there. Glad you have made Planet fall safely and all is well. Have you located CAKE operatives?>>

Scarlett was suddenly up and by the speaker, her eyes wide as Crash spoke into the microphone.

"Beacon is picking up a clear signal Control, will start search straight away."

"That's amazing" Scarlett said "You're talking to Earth." She suddenly looked excited, as if something had dawned on her. "Oh my! You can go back can't you? You're here to rescue people and take them back?"

Crash nodded and was surprised when Scarlett squealed happily.

<<Thank you Crash, keep us informed if you can. We await your reports and safe return.>>

Crash flipped off the Radio switch and looked at Scarlett in surprise.

"You want to leave here?" he asked carefully.

"So much so. The Cephalopod war finished before I was born, and the armies had left. Apart from that one moment in history this has been a strictly one way planet. I'm a creature of two worlds and I'm not welcome on the one fate has me trapped on." She said, hope in her eyes.

"I can't guarantee how welcome you will be on Earth. I'm fairly new to all this myself but there's certainly no harm in giving it a go." He said hoping to sound supportive. "We do need to perform a rescue first however." Crash pointed at the beacon signal. "We get there, we find the sphere and its crew, and then we all go home."

Scarlet looked at the small array of lights arranged like a sun on the dashboard only one of them blinked on and off. Simple enough to follow she thought and looked in the direction the light appeared to indicate. "The Apergy" she murmured to herself before looking up at Crash "Did your friends get dragged through with a Titan?" the question was very direct.

"Yes!" Crash responded, as if being a directly questioned by a superior officer. "Is that bad?" He added less formally as his mind drifted back to the great creature and the storm.

"Well it's certainly not good. If they're still with the Titan then I can't imagine they are doing too well at all. We just have to hope the beast shook them loose, in which case you have to hope their survival skills are top notch. The Apergy aren't known for their hospitality. If we're really lucky your friends are with the Menhune."

"You keep mentioning Menhune - should I be concerned?" Crash asked, hoping to get as many details as possible on the mission ahead long before he faced them.

"Not at all, they're as ancient as the Persians but couldn't be more different. They keep to themselves on the whole, but they also hunt the Titans. Not to kill but to capture. They watch the skies for the storms and when found they try to get to the Titans before anyone else does. Then they spirit them away to the Apergy; great floating islands where the beasts can live without damage to themselves or others."

"They don't kill them?" Crash asked with

surprise.

"Why should they?" Scarlett answered with actual surprise "They haven't done harm to anyone here. Nobody kills the humans that turn up and they are always doing harm. The storms only bring through people while they are in the throes of battle; apparently the violence and the rage of a lot of humans together must activate the Titan seeking storm portals." Scarlett seemed more passionate toward the beasts than she did towards the humans that she shared blood with, and Crash realised he could fully understand why. The war in Europe had shown him a side of human nature he felt best kept under cover, and all Jahannam ever saw of Earth was its warriors.

"So, are all the Human cities warlike?" he asked eventually.

"Can't really say I'm an expert. Historically it's how they all start but time mellows people and seeing as no "Earth born" age or fall ill that's quite a lot of time for some of them." She smiled. "Let's go get your friends, the quicker you find them the quicker we can leave." With these words Scarlett started to undo her tunic, slipping off the many belts and undoing the buttons.

"What are you doing?" Crash asked, prompting Scarlett to hold up his navy blue C.A.K.E coveralls

"If I'm going to be one of you I might as well

look the part." With a single movement she dropped the red tunic from her smooth, dark shoulders.

Crash spun to face away, trying to keep the smile from his face with a cough."When we get back to Earth remind me to tell you about a thing we call modesty." The comment left a confused Scarlett to slip into the spare uniform with a shrug.

"The Apergy will be a harsh environment to explore." She said, doing up the buttons of her new clothes and admiring the fresh new fabric. "The only places with enough space to land this thing safely will be the pathways and clearings of the Titans and I very much doubt you'll want your only way home crushed underfoot. So we'll have to land next to the glimmer zone and find a way to climb up, like everyone else does."

Crash turned back to his new co pilot. "What's the glimmer zone?"

***

Makana of the Menhune watched the skies; it was what her people had always done. She was fairly typical of her tribe in both attitude and appearance. Like most female Menhune she was just over four foot in height with a light amber skin tone and dark hair, little removed from the Polynesian heritage they all originated from. It was strongly believed by all

Menhune, that they had been transported to this new world after a direct ancestral request to their Gods. An unswaying dedication to that belief had kept their bloodline pure.

Makana was trained as a guardian, as were most of her tribe, and her limbs were strong from the exertions of her daily life. Her clothes were simple and scarce covered her body that was adorned with tattoos of those she hunted. Her hair was rich and black; shaved back from her temples so it resembled a dark mane and her eyes were covered by a band of rich red paint that kept both sweat and insects from them. The only thing about her that hinted of vanity towards her appearance was the carved bone hook earring and similar pendant.

She was going against her instincts to attend to the Titans that made her Apergy their home, and had chosen today to sit on a rocky over hang, watching out across the desert that was far below. It was a perfect place to loiter because you could feel the warmth come off the far reaching sands beneath but still have the cool of the green jungle towards your back. She toyed with her blade as she watched the skies and only moved to stay unnoticed in the shadow and shade, although she doubted she was missed or even being sought out. The Jungle Apergy with its beasts was her home, a (fairly) untouched floating island that her tribe monitored ever watchfully. Three Titans now

Welcome to Jahannam

resided between the trees, keeping very much to themselves on the great island sanctuary. Two human tribes were also inexplicably settled within; an uneasy peace resting between them both. The Menhune watched the humans as much as they did the Titans, dealing out ancient judgements when lines were crossed whilst tending to the imprisoned beasts with the same reverence many reserve for Gods; ever watchful for outside interference.

The Menhune knew the titanic creatures and their masters well, historically having dealt with them back on Earth while protecting their island people from the corruption and violence; teaching the Rapa Nui people to build Moai to protect them when the Menhune could not. All this was sang in the history songs of times long before the great banishment, when protection from the titans was needed and sought out. That protection was not wanted here though, there was far too much of an upper hand to be gained from beating the Menhune to a Titan and so a watchful eye and mastery of their unique crafts had turned the Menhune into guardians keeping this new land safe.

It was with the knowledge of this duty that Makana now stood to watch an object in the sky. The shape she had first thought to be a large bird or skyfish was in fact approaching too fast and too straight to be natural; It was an object that was both unknown and flying.

Makana had seen projectiles thrown by the war machines of the human tribes, but you could always see their point of origin however far away, and often you heard the explosive thrust of the thing if that distance was not too great. This shape was almost quiet and had clearly come from a great distance away - too far for even her eyes. It was eventually close enough to see. To Makana's eyes it was as if a crustacean had grown in size and discovered the ability to fly, and for a second she believed it to be a Titan, but the noise was like nothing she had ever heard before. It was certainly crab like if you removed the claws, it even had spindly legs tucked neatly up beneath. As it passed over head she could see it was all manmade and heading off over her jungle

With a click of her tongue Makana was upon her feet and running in the direction it had flown, she knew this was what she had been waiting for.

Welcome to Jahannam

Chapter 11

Inside Harmony, Crash was awestruck.
The Apergy were beautiful.

When he was a child, his mother had once
convinced his father they had needed a break
from the dirt and bustle of the city. His father
had found a custodian to run the Inn for a whole
month, and they had moved up to the Lake
District and the home of an old family friend of
his mothers. It was so nice to see his parents
relaxed and far away from the constant noise of
London life, and for the first and only time
young James was allowed to explore beyond
the sight of his watchful parents. He, of course,
didn't go very far. He was still only a very
young boy, but he had found a small gravel
beach down by the lake and from it he could sit
all day and watch the small boats weave across
the clear waters.
On particularly special days (normally a
Sunday), the lake was empty of traffic and the
water became as still and as reflective as a
mirror. On these days the islands that nestled
tree lined at the lakes heart became suspended
in a mirrored sky until they appeared to float
above the very world itself and on the shore,
with a stick in hand, young James would fight
the many giants he knew must live there.

Now, many years later, the man now
known as Crash approached the very same

apparitions to possibly do just that.

"They're beautiful aren't they?" Scarlett's voice cut through the memory and Crash looked across at his new co pilot, now strapped tightly into his spare C.A.K.E coveralls by the addition of her many belts and the long boots. She'd been pressed against a viewing window for most of the ride and asking many questions about controls the rest of it. It was actually quite nice to have company; the last person Crash had flown tandem with was Lord Percy.

He took his eyes off his co pilot and looked down at the thick Jungle below. The floating islands were big, they had passed over some smaller ones on the way here but in general Crash believed he was looking at land masses well in excess of the area of small countries. They floated at different heights and some over lapped others, water ran from them like rain and the desert directly below would have been alive with verdant greenery if it wasn't in permanent shadow. Crash shivered, aware that many living things liked the cold, wet dark places and very few of them pleasant. This was the area Scarlett had referred to as the glimmer zone and a good place to land. Crash however had other ideas. "There!" he said pointing downwards "A river. We'll just fly up it and land when we see shallows."

Welcome to Jahannam

"These places are far from safe Crash, it's why few people try to get to them." Scarlett seemed concerned for the first time and Crash realised it was possibly one of the few moments she had ever been out of the desert and away from the dangers she knew how to cope with.

"It's possibly more a case of access than real danger." Crash added, trying to sound reassuring. "Places you can't get to always get myths build up around them; as its difficult for someone else to prove you're lying."

"People can get here. " Scarlett began. "They regularly try to plunder the Apergy for their resources or to entrap the Titans to drag back and protect their cities or to use them to smash those of their rivals. That's why the Menhune protect them so fiercely." Scarlett looked at Crash "You're not the only flying craft on Jahannam, you're just not a balloon."

The comments made Crash laugh out loud and jokingly mop his brow with an over dramatic phew. "Thank the stars for that, for a minute there I thought you were going to say they climbed up beanstalks."

Scarlett chuckled too "My father used to tell me that story as a little girl. He found it funny too because of the Apergy. He used to joke when we were hungry that he bet the giants had a lot of bread we could climb up and steal." For a moment she looked thoughtful. "I've never seen so many trees."

116

The comment made Crash look closer at the foliage. This close, he could see the trees were in fact closer in design to fungi. The trunks and branches were certainly wood like but closer in colour and texture to a silver birch than that of an oak, and the leaves were in fact circular platelets of various sizes and shades of green, more like a mushroom's cap. There were birds and animals too sat amongst the branches, that scattered as they flew by. It was all too fast to see but Crash was pretty sure they were creatures and birds he didn't know.

"Look I'm going to take the river route as far up as I can, and then put her down in the shallows. I think having harmony up here with us is a lot safer idea than leaving her down in the glimmer zone. I think the risk of danger is just as great on both options, and this way we're saved a climb." Without awaiting confirmation, Crash turned Harmony back towards the river mouth and with a graceful swerve headed inland.

The journey up river, Crash took as slowly as he could, making sure to keep level with the canopy of trees to ensure the craft fitted without getting trapped on branches. As expected, the river drew life to its banks and at their passing many wonderful creatures were startled by the strange vehicle.

Crash was just debating with himself the safe width of the path they had taken, when the

Welcome to Jahannam

dashboard made a loud ping and took the full attention of both Harmony's occupants. The Sun tracker had one single light lit up and it was right at the heart of the design. Crash found himself checking the trees as he swung Harmony about, causing whirlpools in the river beneath them.

"Do you think its shallow enough?" said Scarlett looking down at the agitated water. Crash didn't answer, just unfolded the Harmony's legs and landed.

It was certainly deeper than was hoped for, the water came up to the Harmony's skirt and the ripples made small waves wash up the sides. They both sat in stillness for a moment watching the water move. Desert life was devoid of water especially in amounts that flowed with the power of a river, and space for all its beauty was very dry. Eventually Crash stood and went to the top hatch "The quicker we find them..." He said as he undid the portal outwards, and was pleased to see Scarlett nod.
***

The two stood on the roof of Harmony, Scarlett with her father's gun drawn but hung at her side, as they both watched the tree line from the safety of their metal island.

"Cover me" Crash said and with a short jump and flick of the switch in his hand, the small cavorite device on his back propelled him across the river, in an epic leap. The landing wasn't as graceful as it could have been but Crash still let out a whoop of joy at the successful test. He turned to see a smiling Scarlett on the distant craft.

"Not bad." She shouted "But how do I get over? And for that matter how do we get everyone else back?"

Crash looked about until he saw what he wanted. One of the mushroom like trees grew close to the bank, its roots showing through the washed away soil. "You may want to stand back." He shouted, and braced himself and started to push. The tree didn't want to move at first but soon the weakened bank started to give, and with a certain satisfactory tearing noise the tree toppled but didn't pull fully from the bank. The upper branches hit just up river of Harmony with a splash, before the current moved them down to rest against the semi submerged craft.

Crash held his palms up with the satisfied smile of a child "Bridge building 101" he laughed.

Scarlett tested the makeshift bridge; it was bouncy in the water but firm enough to walk ashore.

"Of course you could have just jumped me across and saved the tree being drowned." She said derisively when reaching the bank. "And now you have a bridge for anyone who wants onto your craft."

Welcome to Jahannam

Crash felt the edge taken off his success but hoped they wouldn't be on the floating island for long enough for Scarlett to be proved right. "Also what if they're on the other bank." Scarlett said looking across the river seeming to be adding insult to injury, but Crash had already seen what he wanted back when he was stood on harmony.

Walking over to a pile of rocks he wobbled an antenna coming from the top. "Because I saw their homing beacon and ..." he pointed at the trees. "There are scraps of fabric tied to the branches leading us that way." He tugged Scarlett's sleeve "Coverall fabric in C.A.K.E colours."

"That's clever." She said holding one of the bits of fabric, before following after Crash "maybe they will be alive after all."

***

The trees quickly became a tangled mess and what once had looked like a beaten path to the river soon became an obstacle course of entwined roots and branches. Strange alien creatures moved and watched within the branches as the Sun filtered through, casting clearly defined pockets of light and darkness. A small group of birds fed on the ground before them with hair like a kiwi bird rather than feathers, but they burst up into the air at the duos approach to show their wings were like those of bats but with the wonderful iridescent

120

colours of the butterfly. The wonderful spectacle took the attention up to the higher branches where small, bright furred monkeys with multiple eyes and six limbs looked curiously down at the interlopers to their kingdom. The view would have taken Crash's full attention but they then broke into a clearing. It was clearly fresh - the fallen trees still showed whiteness where they were snapped off at the trunk.

"Whatever it was, came in through there...or went out through there?" Scarlett pointed at a broken path in the jungle.

Crash chuckled "I'm guessing it went out...due to the fact it clearly isn't here anymore." He realised Scarlett had gone quiet, her revolver was raised and pointing towards the trees and she slowly crouched down. Crash knew enough to follow suit and looked around him at the trees, realising how exposed they were at present.

"We're being watched." Scarlett whispered.

Crash realised how hot he suddenly felt. They were out of the desert but in the clearing. Without the shade of the trees the Apergy felt hotter than the dry desert. His brow was beaded with sweat and the Uniform he wore was suddenly heavy, uncomfortable and notably lacking a side arm. The tension grew as both the crouched figures watched a place in the

Welcome to Jahannam

trees where more discernible movements could be seen within the gloom .

Makana stepped from the tree line. She had to go against instinct and do so with her knife away to show she was a friend and instead grasped in her outstretched fist strips of blue fabric from a torn uniform.

"Friend." she shouted across the divide but the language was alien to Crash and he heard simply gibberish. Scarlett looked at the man who had saved her from the temple

"Do we trust her?"

Crash had not taken his eyes off the diminutive warrior before them "If she gives us a reason to. At the moment all I see is an armed native with scraps of uniform held in her hand." Scarlett looked back "Oh yeah, so she does. She did shout friend though, that's got to be a good sign."

"You understood her language?" Crash asked, impressed. He had flown alongside French airman for years and still only grasped a percentage of what they were saying.

"I know and speak all languages. She said Friend." Scarlett stood up slowly

"Well you certainly have better schools than we have on Earth then. " Crash stood too, and walked up beside Scarlett. "You best call her over or else she'll be waiting there all day."

Scarlett called out

"We are friends of the Menhune, we do not seek to disturb your Titans. We come seeking our companions, who are lost to us. They wear the material you hold."

"I know of your friends, but they are in danger and request your help for both themselves and my village." The Menhune shouted back, and without being asked she started to walk forward.

"So what's happening?" Crash whispered to Scarlett.

"She says your friends are in trouble, but more worryingly she says so is her village." Scarlett whispered back

"Why are her village's troubles more worrying?" Crash asked confused, he did not see how it was currently of concern.

"Because each and every one of the Menhune warriors can take on a titan single handed and live, and for some reason her whole village is in Danger. If something spooked a group of these guys I'd have cause for concern but something that's endangered their entire village should certainly be troubling both of us." Scarlett's words trailed off as Makana finally reached them.

"They said you would come, they told us you were Englishmen and would free our village from the invaders like the English soldiers freed us all from the cephalopods." With this the Menhune warrior handed over the strips of

Welcome to Jahannam

uniform fabric to Scarlett. "They made me bring their beacon away from the village so you would land away from danger, but now I have found you we will return to save my village and your companions."

Scarlett turned slowly to look at Crash. The concern on her face was enough for him to know something was majorly wrong. "She's been waiting for us, she thinks we are some kind of fighting force from Earth, like my father's. She wants us to save her village from invaders."

"Save her village? I'm not even armed how am I going to save her village? You said they were all warriors , can't they just tell us where our friends are and save their own village?" Crash was angry that he was back in a battle situation and angrier because he was unarmed in a battle situation.

"The English soldiers are revered across Jahannam. Legend spreads and I don't think your friends have done a good job of telling the truth of what kind of rescue was coming for them. " Scarlett said, a hint of anger creeping into her own voice "Let's just go look at the situation and see if we can do anything before we tell this messenger that we just came to get ours but they're on their own regarding the rest."

"Take us to your village." Crash said to the Menhune warrior, making sure his actions spoke louder than his words. Without delay they were off and following the diminutive figure through the broken path of devastation, away from the clearing and Harmony.

***

"I'm going to need your rifle or your revolver." Crash said to Scarlett as they walked and was pleased when without question, she unslung the rifle and handed it across. All military personnel were rigorously drilled in both the projectile and melee use of a standard issue rifle and Crash's training had been no different, despite being issued a service revolver when he got to the front. He trusted the rifle more, it was heavy and practical long after ammo had run out and he had always kept one in the tail section of his plane in case he was downed in enemy territory.

"You're a wiz with language, we'd have been lost without you back there. I very much doubt she speaks English." Crash was honestly still impressed at how fluid the conversation had been, he had seen linguists question enemy troops on the base and even they seemed to struggle to find just the right word in a foreign tongue.

"Polyglot." Was the simple one word answer and Crash was even more impressed.

"My mother knows a few back on Earth." He answered, remembering the studious men who referred to themselves as polyglots

Welcome to Jahannam

because of their skilled understanding and delivery of many languages.

"Maybe on Earth they are different." Scarlett said with a smile, and pulled aside the dark tight curls at the nape of her neck to reveal a barnacle like protrusion on the top of her spine. It truly looked like two stone grey crustaceans were attached to the skin as tight as they would be to the hold of a ship, one above the other but fused together at the base as if they were one.

"What is it?" Asked Crash concerned. "Does it hurt?" Then remembering where he was, "Oh my stars, I'm sorry, is it part of you being Hitherian?"

Scarlett laughed and got shot a glance by the serious looking warrior they followed "No it isn't me and it doesn't hurt; although if someone talks too long it can tickle and become warm. It's the male half of a predator from the glimmer zone. They attach themselves to a host and wait, so that when the female half calls out - a great nasty creature that's rooted to the spot and always hungry - the host hears their own language and believes one of their own is calling out in the swamp, possibly stuck and hungry. They go close, and whammo! They're lunch. " Scarlett was enjoying the look of shock on Crash's handsome face, so she continued. " People gather up the males and sell them at markets. Attach one to the base of your neck and you can understand any language that's spoken to you. If you've heard it before you even have the knowledge to speak it back. Handy little things."

Crash shook his head at the marvels and wonders a new world would clearly unveil to him. He was also aware it was getting cooler as the sun was going down.

Makana held up her hand and crouched, Crash and Scarlett did likewise. They followed after her until they were on the top of a rise looking across at the Menhune village as the sun shone its last golden rays across its many buildings.

Welcome to Jahannam

Chapter 12

The Menhune village was built on a jutting rock structure that had been carved over the years into steps down the front, and smoothed on the back and sides into a non climbable wall. It could only be approached from the front and from this direction there was a great hole in the ground. This hole descended to the glimmer zone beneath and was crossed only by one strong, wide, rope bridge. Crash realised the geological significance of the structure immediately. On Earth, similar things happened; hard rock beds moved upwards creating cliffs and rocky outcrops, while the hole they left filled with water creating lakes. However, here there was no earth beneath and the hole remained just that; a hole. It made for a fantastically defendable structure and the Menhune had carved it so it was also a fine place to live, with their houses built up on the steps so streets were formed but no view was obstructed.

Of course that would have been the case if this was indeed a defended area, but it was clear this was not the case. Armoured figures were herding the Menhune into one or two of the buildings as the day became night. It was obvious the entire village was captured by interlopers, but there was more to interest

Crash's eye than the imprisoned. Chained to the floor before the steps of the village and behind the great abyss, was the Titan he had seen back on Earth. It thrashed and pulled at its bonds but could not break free, and its efforts had clearly worn it down into a tired and dying creature in bondage. However, the best was yet to come for Crash. As the sun dipped below the horizon and the sky went through the shades of sunset, the silhouette of the missing cavorite sphere was revealed to be chained to the same area. It bobbed above everything like a balloon, but it was still attached and operational. Crash's thoughts were interrupted by the whispered words of Scarlett.

"Persians." She almost spat the name there was so much venom in her voice.

Crash tried to study the armoured figures better, but the twilight made it difficult. He could see well during the day and his sight adjusted at night but the fading light of dusk made it almost impossible. He pulled out a pair of battered old opera glasses his mother had given him to play with as a child. He loved them for their practicality and size, and took them everywhere with him from that day forth. The armoured figures slowly came into focus and Crash was instantly startled by their appearance. They were indeed suits of armour, but that appeared to be all they were. Metal bodies jointed like that of men but clearly holding nothing inside. Their heads were either armoured helmets in a Persian style that glowed dimly from within, or were clear glass and contained human skulls surrounded by a soft luminous mist.

"What has happened to them?" Crash whispered, not taking his eyes off the strange, bone and metal puppets.

"They're Persians." Scarlett answered. "Hellish creatures that worship their Titan God and follow their one true King. They strip away all that is good until they are left with just the serviceable components . I've never known them to make it to the Apergy though, they normally concentrate on the desert cities and the Hitherian as a rule. No wonder the Menhune were easily overthrown. They cannot be killed in the traditional sense."

"What do you mean they can't be killed in the traditional sense?" He asked as he watched. "It's all about shaking them completely from their connection to the mortal. They are like a mist but they must hold always onto something physical as an anchor. Each one of those creatures has something of their original selves still contained with the mists. It could be ashes, but is more likely to be a bone or tooth. The leaders must hold onto their skulls to not be considered commoners, and the royalty... well they keep as much as they can." Scarlett said, wishing she did not know as much as she did about them.

"But there's nothing to them. How can these creatures be the Persians of Earth?" Crash asked. His question went no further. The world went dark.

***

Crash awoke to find himself on hard ground, bound at the hands and feet, looking up at the night sky. He could smell the musk of the great titan close by, but it was silent save for its heavy laboured breathing.

"What's going on?" He whispered, and was glad when a feminine groan sounded beside him.

"Ambushed?" Scarlett's groggy voice replied "How did we not hear them?"

"Persian's can be as quiet as mist if they slip off their shells, but are still able to lift a concussive rock or two. They probably saw the sunset glinting off your spyglasses. They would have been upon us in a second." Scarlett wasn't judging, her tone was matter of fact, but the conversation ended as suddenly stood over them both as a metal marionette sculpted to look intimidating and fierce. It bent and grabbed each of them roughly by the throat, and pulled them choking to their unsteady feet.

The creature let them go as a sinister glow behind the hollow eyes of its helmet faded, and they were faced by three more of these strange

Welcome to Jahannam

metal puppets, each subtly different and yet uniform in design.

To Crash's eyes they were instantly identifiable as soldiers and that meant they had orders not to kill the hostages or it would be done already. In their presence he felt strangely safe, but it was the figure that was stood between them that made him feel queasy. Clearly this was their boss; their superior. A complete human skeleton bleached so white that the bones shone, dressed in a stylish black silk uniform with gold trim. But what made this apparition disturbing was strapped to the front of the skull by a black ribbon; a ceramic human mask, sculpted with an expression of benign wisdom that was both beautiful and hideous to behold.

"And so it seems we just keep getting more of you." The creatures lyrical words did not move the mask, but sounded like the air itself had spoken and as it did so wisps of mist billowed gently from the concealed skull. It moved fluidly towards its captives turning its head in an almost birdlike manner to inspect its prize. Crash had expected jerkiness to its motion, and had hoped he would understand the words it spoke. To him though, it simply looked and sounded ancient and archaic.

It reached out for Scarlett, a tight glove held the bony fingers like dark skin and it ran them sensually down her cheek.

"Don't touch her." Crash shouted, and the figure snapped its head around to look at the bound man.

"I hear a feisty one, but unfortunately with the voice of the muddied barbarians. I don't understand you little warrior and I doubt you understand me." It whispered menacingly in ancient Persian.

"He told you to take your hands off me." Scarlett said in reciprocated Persian, her voice loaded with quiet menace despite the situation.

"Finally." The creature said raising its hands up and out like a preacher who had seen the light. "An educated Barbarian, with I'm guessing, a working knowledge of the machine." He pointed at the floating sphere. "Oh how I have waited for you. You see I needed someone I could understand but what I don't need is more...feisty" and with a sudden strike his hand hit Crash full in the chest. With feet bound the pilot could not keep his balance, and with a surprised look on his face Crash toppled backwards and disappeared through the hole.

"Nooo!" Scarlett shouted at the shock of the action. "You've killed him." Angry tears filled her eyes.

"I do hope so, everything here seems to take so long to die." It replied. With this, the creature looked at the bound titan. "Bring her."

Welcome to Jahannam

At his words two of the soldiers grabbed Scarlett and lifted her kicking and thrashing between them.

They walked up the steps past many more of the metal soldiers that appeared to either be garrisoned, or guarding buildings in which she assumed Menhune were imprisoned. They were certainly all waiting for something important to happen. Scarlett was dragged past all of them and into the largest building, where a fire crackled at its heart illuminating two more humans dressed in the blue uniform, although the man's was heavily torn and he himself was bruised and beaten. Scarlett was thrown down between them.

"I'm sure you must have a lot of catching up to do. Make it quick and don't leave out the detail of the man's death. I shall return to question you all when my tools are ready again." With this he moved to the far side of the room and started sorting through a selection of things that rattled and clinked like metal.

"Oh, my dear, are you okay?" said the woman in polished English; quickly checking Scarlett for wounds. The man was less friendly and more down to business, he spoke quickly and hushed, his voice cracked with pain at the effort.

"How many of there are you? We were hoping the rescue would come soon. We tried to get word to you with one of the natives, told her to hide our beacon away from the site and not to bring you here without an army. Did the message get through?" he said with panic in his voice.

"It was just Captain Jackson, myself and the Menhune warrior who came. I don't know where she is, but they killed the Captain on our arrival." Scarlett whispered back trying to keep the emotion from her voice. She hadn't known Crash long but she felt his loss strongly.

"They only sent two?" The man said, looking at the woman. "I told you your mother would not risk lives, even to save you." He turned back to Scarlett "So how did you get here and what breakthrough have they concocted to save us. I've worked out from the stars where we are and without a damn fine vessel we're not all going back. We're certainly not going back in the Darwin, she's too badly damaged."

Scarlett tried to ignore the man's aggressive tone and took a breath. She had to tell the humans everything; it was only fair. "Your mother didn't send two." She carried on quickly as the man's relief looked like it would interrupt her. "She only sent Captain Jackson."

"Who the hell are you then?" The man said angrily

"Calm your temper Byron and let the lady talk." The woman's voice was soft and had an

Welcome to Jahannam

instant effect on her husband

"My name is Scarlett Byrne. Crash, I mean Captain Jackson, made me his co pilot after I rescued him from being eaten by Morn. He has a special ship he says can get you all home."

"Oh great a rookie futurenaut goes all Martian princess on us." Byron angrily spouted, turning his head towards the fire. The wife was more understanding and smiled at Scarlett.

"My husband doesn't mean his anger. He is trapped and frightened, so forgets his manners. You said Captain Jackson made you his co-pilot, does this mean you can control the craft he has?"

Scarlett shook her head "No! But I know how to get back to it, if we can escape, maybe one of you will work out the controls, although his vessel looks different to yours."

Byron turned back, his anger seeming to have passed "Okay, maybe we can salvage this situation. We just need a plan of escape. Can you understand the natives or maybe even these monstrosities? They all talk, but only the masked one talks directly to us. We believe its name to be Corvus. It believes itself to be some kind of prince, but beyond that we have nothing."

The name made Scarlett's blood run cold. Whispers told of The Persian King, but they also spoke of his children; the princes and princesses, each as evil as their father, each in charge of their own citadel and army moving progressively out of the deserts. Out of all of their many evils one name stood out in tales designed to make a child look beneath their bed before sleep, and that was the name of Crown Prince Corvus, the pirate prince, with his fleet of balloon ships.

"I understand all their words and can speak them too. I urge you, whatever Corvus asks of us, we must comply. He will want to know the workings of your craft and now he knows I understand him he will torture whoever he thinks is the weaker of the two of you, so that the other will talk. We have no guarantees he won't anyway. If we keep him happy, he may let us live long enough to escape."

The words were cut off by the sound of metal being plunged into the hot coals of the fire.

"Have you had chance to catch everyone up, little sparrow. Because I want to know how your craft flies before my irons are hot enough to remove an eye."

***

Crash had fallen, that was true. The sudden shock put his heart in his throat, but he had an ace up his sleeve thanks to the mechanics back at C.A.K.E. The still very much present device on his back when Corvus pushed him over, was a cavorite chute just in case Harmony had somehow malfunctioned. It was designed to

Welcome to Jahannam

activate if plummeting, so if Crash bailed out he
could go unconscious and still be safe, as there
was no need for buttons to be pressed for
activation. A weak charge would be sent
through a cavorite solution within, and although
it wouldn't stop his fall it would impeded its
speed to a survivable landing. It turned out to
work just fine and although he landed in the
moist cold earth of the Glimmer zone, arms and
legs still bound, he was far from dead.

The struggle now was to escape. Crash thrashed
around in the slime, balling himself up so he
could slip his bound wrists beneath his feet, and
with his hands free he started working on the
knot of rope binding his ankles. In the half light
and with the muddy slime caking the rope with
filth, it was proving more difficult than he
hoped, and now he was aware of the strange
sucking noises. Something was approaching
fast. Crash turned his head to see a yellow grey
octopus type creature sliding through the ooze
in which he lay. He called it an octopus because
the bulbous head undulated in shape but
somehow always managed to keep the large
pale eyes focused on its possible prey. The
tentacles were in fact a skirt of corpulent flesh
that stretched tendril-like along the ground
looking for hard points to grasp to propel itself
forward by, and things pulsed deep inside it. As
their eyes met it stopped, as if by being still

Crash would lose sight of the stealthy assassin. Both were still for an exceptionally long time, but then as if the creature could wait no more it propelled itself at an alarming speed. The next moment happened in a flash; Crash freed his legs and stood quickly. Holding the rope from his ankles in both hands he whipped it around at the oozing creature, the great knots still in one end, and it made heavy contact with the beast. It tore through its flesh like a fist through wet lard. The yellow grey exterior was quickly obscured by a bright, foul smelling liquid from within, and the creature seemed to deflate like a burst balloon full of semolina. Suddenly the ground around the creature was alive with small muddy brown crabs that scurried across its surface to feast. Crash almost gagged but he covered his mouth to avoid the worst of the smell, and used his teeth to unbind his wrists.

Weapon less, Crash used his hand binding to make a larger knot around the rope from his legs, giving him a passable (if somewhat impractical) rope flail. It was going to be a long night, but he had to try and head out from beneath the Apergy above and get back to the ship and Scarlett.

***

Unaware Crash was alive and thinking of mounting some kind of rescue, Scarlett was trying to formulate a plan of her own. She did this by buying time, translating Byron's words

Welcome to Jahannam

regarding the Cavorite sphere to the ever attentive Persian prince. She, however, had realised the Prince was at a loss as to the right questions to ask. So he was vague, which was good, but the scientist was too easy on the information. The conversation was going something along the lines of the Prince asking a question, based on his limited understanding of the potentials of Cavorite, followed by a lengthy answer from Byron that not only dealt with the prince's question but also filled him in on the things he didn't know to ask. This was followed by Scarlett just translating back the answer to the question that was asked. This way everyone got what they wanted and the conversation moved at a snail's pace.

Eventually the conversation was interrupted when a soldier walked into the room, one of the ones with a bleached skull beneath a domed glass helmet. As it entered it saluted his prince with a double tap to the chest.

"The Titan is about to breathe its last, Prince Corvus." The soldier said with a voice like metal vibrating.

"At last. It held on well, but my sister knows her poisons. I want to see the light go out in its eyes and then I will select a soldier I believe worthy enough to wear its body." The prince had glee in his misty voice

"We do still have the remnant with us Sire." The soldier was clearly reminding his lord and master of information that he had forgotten, but in a way that made it seem like he was answering an unasked question.

"Ah yes the remnant. We will infect the body with all the proper ceremony and then I shall imprint myself upon it." Corvus turned on his captives, "Such a shame you will not get to see the birth of a demi-rot, but I think you should stay here and draw me plans. I will return to my citadel with not only my titan, but also with the power of flight. The citizens of Persia deserve better than my father." He pointed one of the gloved skeletal fingers at a table where parchment, ink and pens waited, and then back at the fire where the instruments still glowed white "But I am not a monster, I will give you the choice of either." And with this he swept from the building.

Scarlett stood and hopped to the door to see two soldiers had been left standing either side of the entrance. It was an easily defendable building with openings only to the front, so it was also easily guarded. She hopped back. "Byron, start writing up plans to the sphere he case he comes back. You... sorry, I didn't get your name."

"It's Alice." Said the woman with a smile "I should have introduced myself."

"Alice. You untie me, then we're going to use those blades and pokers to make a hole through that wall." She pointed at a side wall that was

Welcome to Jahannam

furthest from the fire and in a small amount of darkness.

"Isn't that a bit risky?" added Byron, barely looking up from his plans "He could come back in moments."

"I doubt very much if he will. They are going to see the Titan die, and then they're going to infect it with another Titan. Could take awhile. I'm guessing at the worst we'll be undisturbed until morning. At best we could have till noon tomorrow." Scarlett grabbed an instrument from the fire. The handle was certainly warm, but the blade that had been in the flames glowed white and distorted the air. "I don't intend to be here when he returns."

Alice grabbed a twisted spike from the flames, and both women crouched before the far wall and started working away at the rock from which it was carved.

"Why does he want the Titan dead?" asked Alice as they scored lines into the wall. Scarlett was reminded that the people she was currently with had no knowledge of the planet's history or politics so ingrained into the people of Jahannam. "The Persians - they're our captives - are fanatical followers of both their King and the Titan they worship as a deity. The Titan is known only as the Rot and lives beneath the main Persian citadel, the throne of their King. The Persians realised many centuries ago that they did not succumb to age or infection, and several lifetimes of no change often leads to madness. The King went first so it seems. It's said he could hear the voice of the Titan beneath them and it spoke profound words of religious wisdom. So in this madness he sacrificed himself to the Rot. Laid himself out on an ornate lattice bed and had parts of the Rot brought up in gilded jars and spread on his naked body like oil. The Rot failed to kill him in such a strange application, so the King declared himself imprinted on the titan and declared that now he too was a god. With this he left his sacrificial bed and wrote down the words of the Rot as they were said to him. The rot was demanding sacrifice greater than the livestock it was fed regularly. So he brought forward his palace guard, and placing them in a feeding pit he allowed the rot to pour right in on them. As the rot drained away back to its lair, ghostly mists of the ten palace guards remained. You see here on Jahannam the transported cannot die by anything other than an act of catastrophe or violence. This sacrifice was somehow one of devotion and love to the King; the bodies were gone but the guard remained with just a few bits of their undigested bone. For years they acted as a symbol of piety, these disembodied mists, but soon it was found they could interact too, lift things with their will alone. Freed from their bodies they became strong. The King had suits of hinged armour made for them. They inhabited these like new skins and were indestructible.

The king of course had never washed the religious offering from his body and over the years he slowly rotted, but his decomposition was seen as an act of extreme faith and what was good for their beloved king was good for them. Persians sacrificed themselves to the food pits or took part in elaborate year long ceremonies where they were stripped back to their very skeletons. The freed souls animated these skeletons or had beautiful ones made from carved wood or cast metals. It was only the transported that could survive this, the Persians born here would rub themselves with the oils of the rot and decompose as they lived, an act of piety ending in death." Scarlett stopped. The blade had cooled and now it scratched inefficiently at the rock. She looked up to see both Byron and Alice were wrapped in her story, faces full of shock.

"That's horrible." Said Alice finally.

"Worst things have been done for both Kings and religions, so my father said" Alice Said returning back to the fire and swapping her blade for a new white hot instrument.

"But why kill the Titan here and infect it?" Byron asked

"Because he's creating a new god to rival his fathers." Was Scarlett's simple reply.

Chapter 13

It was true; Corvus had planned the downfall of his father for what would have been generations of a mortal life. His father encouraged the deception and machinations of his son, as he did with all his children. It kept them fresh and hungry for power.

Corvus, however, was in it for the long game. He knew his father had many supporters, but a lot of that support came from his connection to the Rot and Corvus had told him so. This had resulted in a public and humiliating display where the King had given Corvus a tiny off cut of the Rot, a sentient bonsai Titan to call his own.

The Prince was not one for humiliation, and he vowed that day to turn the gift against his father.

It was now that vow was about to become a reality. When the remnant had been handed to Prince Corvus, his father had officially carried out the ancient ceremonies employed for the bonding of a titan permanently to a host master. After this, the titan could never have another master and the master could never have another Titan. The King had publicly bound his son to an insignificant morsel of the great power his father controlled. The great Titan before them was still young and unclaimed by anyone. It,

Welcome to Jahannam

however, could not be claimed by the prince who was bound to his remnant; but Corvus had discovered another ceremony. A ceremony in which the Remnant would barter with the dying Titan for its continued life, a symbiotic process in which they would become one. In doing so they would become Corvus's.

Corvus said his incantations over the dying beast, with each of his spoken oaths echoed back by the pious soldiers.

The great titan rolled its eyes, a great black tongue licking it's foam flecked lips and flopping weakly from its jaw as it listened, and felt the powerful chants. The beast was like a great mountain gorilla, devoid of hair with flesh like the blubber of a whale and deep grey in colour, laced with livid white scars and gouged holes. Its head was almost malformed in its simplicity; no nose, tiny round earlobes, but a great jutting jaw and heavy brow that almost dwarfed the small eyes it protected. Along its body great curving channels ran and from their depths a fierce fiery light emanated, but as the poison did its work on the hulking brute the light dimmed until it almost died completely.

Corvus walked forward, holding aloft a vessel as he came, the remnant housed inside. Its agitated activity within its confinements was in direct contrast to the inevitable stillness of the great titan it approached. Corvus stood beside the beast just below its jaw and tipped the jar forward until what looked like putrid pus rolled and spilled forth into the titans open mouth. As the last dregs oozed forth Corvus ran his gloved fingers through it, and on the exposed temples of his skull, drew lines that left wet traces on the white bone.

Then he retreated back and continued his chant to be echoed by his soldiers.

The Titan fell still, it was as if death had finally taken it. The incantations continued almost with a renewed joy.

***

    Inside their prison, Scarlett and Alice had broken through. They just needed to make the hole big enough for everyone to squeeze out. Scarlett stopped digging and placed her hand on Alice's arm to stop her too. The building fell instantly quiet and they all listened intently. Something had changed in the air. The soldiers by their door had gone from a quiet vigil and were now chanting along with the ceremony below. The sound of all the combined voices was drifting up from the courtyard, the pace steadily quickening as religious fervour was taking hold.

"We need to hurry" said Scarlett, getting back to the job at hand but with vigour returning to

her actions. "Byron! Help us they won't be
fooled now by your working."

Byron was still looking worriedly at the
door and the sound of the alien chanting.
"Byron! Focus" Scarlet hissed. Snapped from
his cold panic, Byron grabbed a tool from the
fire and joined the women at the wall. Adopting
a levering action to their scrapping and
chipping until a largish section fell away, they
all dropped what they were doing and pushed
through into the open air beyond.

"We need to get back to Harmony." Scarlett
whispered. "We can't go past the courtyard,
we'll be seen. So we need to climb down the
walls."

"What are they doing?" Alice asked, her
attention fixed on the small cluster of metal
troops and their skeletal leader.

"No idea, but it can't be good. Now
climb." Scarlett instructed pointing over the
edge of the stepped terrace.

"It's almost smooth." Byron complained
looking for hand holes before starting his
descent.

Scarlett looked over and cursed, the wall
down had indeed been smoothed off to prevent
attack. The same was also true of the Hitherian
city walls, to prevent Morn attack. She
remembered however climbing those self same
walls as a child and checked this wall for the
same tell tale holes. To smooth something you

have to be able to climb it and often that was done by peg holes; little round holes where strong pegs would be placed so a board could be laid across as platforms for the workers. Without the pegs they were only climbable by the strongest and nimblest of climbers, and Scarlett doubted Byron was up for that. His wife maybe, but the scholarly space explorer was certainly designed for desk and blackboard work. She looked around amongst the detritus at the top of the wall and what looked like a pile of discarded firewood caught her eye. "Grab some of those long sticks each and follow me. It's going to be slow going but it's the only way." With this she leant over the wall and pushed a peg in the top hole of the wall, and then another below it. Using these she swung down on the wall and dangled, before using her new position to put in another peg lower down and move her weight to that peg. Each of the three pegs she had now placed stuck out from the wall like little perches and she sat on the bottom most rung.

"I'm not doing that." Said Byron with genuine fear to his voice. "It's madness."

"Just go." Alice almost scolded, aware her husband would rather stay and face imprisonment and torture than risk anything that might result in actual death. The words fired up something in him and he lowered himself onto the first perch as Alice looked nervously from him to the hole they had made in the wall and the possible sudden appearance of a guards face.

Soon all three of them were cleverly scaling down the sheer surface. Scarlett in the lead finding lower holes and jamming in the long pegs, Byron sweating profusely in the middle easing himself slowly down and Alice at the top following on behind. Eventually the pegs they had brought ran out and it was Alice's job to remove the last peg she was on and pass that down; it slowed them considerably but also saw fit to cut off anyone following them as they took away the hand holds.

It was going to be a battle, but it needed to be done to reach safety.

***

Crash too had a battle on his hands. The glimmer zone had thrown up challenges, and creatures all desperate to make a meal of him and stop him getting out from beneath the Apergy. Now he stood hoping to face his final foe. He was bleeding from an arm wound and his clothes were torn and mud encrusted. He held the rope flail in his left hand and what had been the almost metal-hard spike of some kind of giant insect in his right. The Creature before him seemed rooted to the spot and who could blame it, this close to the edge of the Apergy. Water flowed like a curtain and the ground was a thick ooze even Crash was struggling to move in. On seeing the static creature, Crash was originally going to just walk past the foe, but something flexed beneath the mud and he sensed a trap. So he opted that he would go for the more direct route of through the beast itself. He scanned it for a weakness as he approached. The creature seemed to be a giant mouth like pod, and he was reminded of the pod he had torn himself from on arrival. Could this be the same thing, but alive and in situ? Or was it just a similar species from the same genus? It was constantly making weird cooing and burbling noises and Crash remembered Scarlett's words of the polyglot female luring her prey in with the help of its translating parasitic counterpart, and he wondered if this was it and how it sounded without the parasitic male. He was about to charge when behind him a root like tentacle erupted from the thick mud, wrapped around his waist and lifting him in the air like a doll, propelled him forward towards the opening mouth. Crash saw in the inside of the beast's mouth a pulsing purple sack of what must have been all its organs, protected by a hard fibrous net. He lowered the metal-hard spike and allowed the speed to carry him devastatingly forward like a knight of old, lance at the ready.

The squeal as the sack ruptured was painful to the ears, but the root let Crash drop. He ran past

Welcome to Jahannam

the creature stumbling into the mud and there, in the detritus of its ejected scraps, his thoughts were confirmed on its identity. The parasitic males clearly fed or gained sustenance from the parts the female didn't need and the double barnacle like creatures were all around him. Picking one up Crash was reminded of a millipede, but he put all bad thoughts from his mind and placed it on the back of his neck as close to where he had seen Scarlett's. For a second the sensation of having a spider scurry on his flesh was present and he had to resist brushing it off, but then a quick sharp pain was followed by a great heat building in the back of his neck. Crash cried out in serious pain. Despite all his other injuries from the glimmer zone this was the worst. Lights appeared to explode before his eyes and a ringing built in his ears, as a taste like vomit rose in his burning throat. He spat but nothing came up. Then, as quick as it all started, it stopped. A cooling relief not only soothed the symptoms but a surge ran down his spine and adrenalin made his heart jump, chasing fatigue from his bones.

Gathering himself together Crash emerged from beneath the Apergy into what felt like the lightening sky just before dawn. The chill of even the night time desert was warmer than the cold of the glimmer zone. He looked up at the island above him and wondered how he would return to its plateau again to hopefully continue his mission. As he did so, he saw something that made him smile. Beside the cascades of water that fed the glimmer zone, there were vines. Strong knotted together vines benefiting from the constant cool water from above.

"Looks like you have your beanstalk." He said to himself as he grabbed and tested the living ropes for firm attachment. With a couple of heaves Crash was up and climbing, finding loops and tangles to aid him

It was certainly a distance, but it was going to be an easy ascent if he kept his strength.

***

Scarlett and the futurenauts reached the bottom of the wall as the sun was climbing into the morning sky. Byron had become pale and silent after a couple of slips, but it was a nice change from his bellyaching. Scarlett couldn't help but think they would have cleared the wall quicker without him. However, now they were at the bottom they just needed to circumnavigate the Menhune village, find the broken path and head back to the clearing. Once there they could follow the tied fabric path back to the river and Harmony, then Alice and Byron could work out a way home. The thought spurred Scarlett on and the trio were off at a pace into the jungle.

As they ran they came level with the ceremony, and they couldn't help but watch despite themselves.

Welcome to Jahannam

The morning sun's rays edged across the courtyard by the abyss, first lighting up the Persian soldiers with Corvus at their head and then the great apelike beast of a Titan. Even from this distance you could see the creature was again breathing. The tracks on its flesh that once glowed with fire now had a pale luminous hue about them and the skin of the creature was looking pallid and sickly. The eyes rolled about, but rather than the dark primal anger of before they were yellow wide orbs that bulged alarmingly and swirled with liquid within. As the sun's rays reached the creature's chest, it coughed and spat forth great fleck of luminous spittle that sizzled in the air and clung to its body. It moved one arm and the chain that had bound it shattered into broken links, as if it was now possessed by a greater strength than it had ever known.

"Run!" whispered Scarlett trying to tear her own eyes away from the unfolding rebirth of the Titan and spur the others on to fleeing.

They picked up pace, stumbling through the coarse undergrowth to get back to the broken path and a way home before they were discovered.

Corvus had stopped the chants to watch the Titan rise. He applauded the first roar as it found its feet. His father's titan was so quiet, so sedated; an oozing destructive mass of necrotic flesh, but this creature before him was a beast. A titan worthy of a conqueror; a raging hulk of pestilence that would win this prince a crown. This excursion to the Apergy had bought two prizes to the would-be King - a body in which to host his growing remnant and the power of flight in something with more impact than a balloon ship. The Titan bent towards Corvus and over its shoulder the prince saw the tethered sphere; a sphere that his prisoners would unlock the secrets to. Corvus patted the jaw of the Titan like a master praises his hounds. His father's ritual had been profound in bonding the two together, and now Corvus had given his Titan a new body.

"My father has his Rot but I have a Blight to cast upon the land... That is what I shall call you." He turned to his soldiers and threw up his hands, "Bow before your new God. Bow before Blight and praise him." The soldiers fell to their knees and gave up thanks to their Prince and his Titan.

Corvus almost cackled in his joy, but he held in the madness long enough to see three figures clambering over the fallen trees of the jungle behind his praising troops. He was about to order them to leave their shells and fetch the prisoners back when he laughed and turned back towards his Titan.

"Mighty Blight, my prisoners feel they can just

Welcome to Jahannam

run from my benevolent power. Bring me back two and have your fill of the third." He pointed at the fleeing figures.

Scarlett saw the gesticulation towards them and the great beast cast its terrible jaundiced eyes in their direction, as she helped Byron climb up the slope. The titan rushed forward as praying soldiers scattered and with a bound he leapt the abyss. The creature faltered however at the lip; its jump possibly wasn't as great as it once was and it had to find balance. This was all the motivation Scarlett, Alice and Byron needed to run for all their worth.

Chapter 14

Finding its footing the Blight focused once again on its prey, it could feel the desires of a new heart within its own and it now wanted to please those more than any others. Those desires were to chase down these tiny fools who believed they were better than a Prince, more cunning and slippery than Corvus, but they had failed and now Blight was to become his righteous anger, his angel of destruction and his might.

Blight felt different. His life had started in turmoil and pain, buried deep beneath the soil and growing into a fearsome beast hidden from the world. The anger finally seeping down to him, the blood saturating the soil and drawing him hungry to the surface , to the constant pounding noise, the pull of misery and death. He burst out into a grey sky lit by flashes of light, and all around he heard cries of terror and panic as the small creatures in drab grey stumbled about and tried to hurt him with things that flashed and tore through him. Great bales of wire entwined his limbs, biting deep into his flesh and slicing his skin, rending deep wounds in fresh muscle. His hunger was intense as he grabbed great handfuls of the little running folk and pressed them screaming into his mouth, biting down so they popped and

Welcome to Jahannam

crunched between his teeth and rolled sweet over his tongue.

Then the storm came. The cold wind that pulled at him and tried to guide him away from the morsels, the sweet treats that sated his appetite. He fought against it, but the more he refused to give into its will the stronger it became. Flashes of blinding light robbing him of sight, great rolls of sound deafening to ears used to hearing filtered by the many layers of earth. The flying things were then present in the storm, they flashed like the little running things but the flashes hurt more, dug deeper into his powerful body with heat and pain. So he struck out, grabbed them from the sky and threw them at each other so they burst in great balls of fire. But then something hurt its foot, tangled its good arm in chains, and the storm pulled it so hard it couldn't feel itself at all. Then it was lost. Moving in a void of confusion and swirling blue light. It crashed down into the trees that broke beneath it, but still the thing held its arm, the strange floating ball. The titan had grabbed it and thrust it down hard, but it shot up and pulled its arm so badly even the beast had to yell in pain. It forced it down again and it shot up a second time, striking it in the face and dislodging teeth. So it grabbed it again and slammed it into the ground, striking it again and again until the ground tore chunks from it and it sank deeper and deeper until only a tiny dome remained above the soil. The beast had snorted with perceived victory and the defeat of its enemy but then it opened, and two figures climbed from it and ran for the trees. It went to pursue, to eat and fill its belly with the sweet taste of them, but the smaller figures came and they were singing and the beast felt tired and it wanted to curl up and heal.

***

It had no idea how long it had slept but when it awoke it was alone in a clearing surrounded by trees, it looked for the dome and the little figures, but where it had been was now a little hole; an indent in the ground in which grass already grew. The rage had gone and its many wounds had healed too. The chains and painful wire was missing from its limbs and it felt no hunger or cold, it was as content as it had been in the cold ground. Now the warmth of the sun was on its face, and all around it creatures moved without fighting.

It stayed in the clearing for some time watching the sun move across the heavens, the light fade and returns then fade again. Then the metal figures came, it could taste them on the air; they weren't sweet, they were bitter and it didn't like them and how they made it grow angry, but the angry felt good. It wanted to smash the metal men, but then, like the figures before they started to flash and the flash hurt more than the men in the mud and each flash

Welcome to Jahannam

made it cold and dizzy and for the first time ever the creature understood death and it was frightened.

The next parts came fleeting. It was dragged through the trees, breaking them, hurt by their shards but it couldn't find the energy to resist. It saw a battle around where the metal men fought the singing people, and many of the singers died or were thrown to their deaths. Then it was just laid out cold on the ground as the bitter metal figures watched silently, watched the creature die.

Then the songs had started again. These songs didn't make the creature tired, they made it fight, they made it want to live, and they made it angry and full of rage. They taught it to fight again and then he came, the bone white prince, the one whose name was Corvus and he gave it strength and purpose and it clawed itself back from a cold dark tunnel that was death and roared back to life. Because of him.

And now he wanted it to fetch and to kill, and it was fine with that.

Blight crested the rise, and there were the figures it had been sent to retrieve in the name of its lord. Two of them were from the sphere, the ball from the storm that had entangled it and brought it here. It would kill one of them. It would be justice.

***

Scarlett tried to run behind the others as a way of pushing them forward, but although she was opting to take the rear she was also aware she was unarmed, the feeling of being weapon less hit her suddenly very hard. She'd not just been disarmed by the Persians, she'd had her father's things taken from her. His revolver and the rifle were both gone and it felt for the first time that he wasn't there to fight by her side.

She'd always had a strong sense of herself and had been alone for a long time, but she could always convince herself her father was still there with her by the weight of his gun. She hesitated, and it was in that moment that the Blight appeared over the rise. Scarlett had never seen the Titan moving but could tell something had changed; he already looked corrupted and wrong.

She wasn't going to let the fact she had no guns mean she would be defenceless. Scarlett looked about and saw only broken trees. Nothing to slow the beast, it had after all broken the trees itself, so she stood her ground. She just had to earn the Futurenauts enough time to escape. They deserved to make it back home whereas this by rights was her home, and she was going

Welcome to Jahannam

to prove its inhabitants could look after their guests.

Blight swiped a big hand around in a devastating arc. Scarlett didn't stand a chance, the beast snatched her off the ground and had her held tight in his great paw and he didn't even stop his charge forward.

Alice saw their protector disappear, but Byron hadn't turned once. He was fixed on where they were heading. Alice and he hadn't seen the clearing since they had dug up the damaged sphere and helped carry it back to the Menhune village to fix, something that had taken months and was almost complete when the Persians came and imprisoned everyone. They had only one quick chance to see the path through the jungle from the clearing and to the possible escape in the new C.A.K.E craft.

It had seemed a sensible idea to get the Menhune warrior to carry the homing beacon away from the village so its landing didn't alert the Persians to its presence and possible rescue, but now running away from a Titan with his lungs about to burst, he was wishing it had been placed closer. It was only Alice's scream that made him turn at all.

To Byron's eyes the titan was as unholy as any creature could be. C.A.K.E. had sent the married couple around the solar system, and Alice had been a fantastic strong armed negotiator and mediator for many planets and races. Byron had acted as scientific advisor only, trying hard to keep his growing revulsion at the creatures they dealt with hidden deep inside. The call to act as war correspondents for his own kind had been a blessing, and he had begged Alice to join the allied forces. Then this creature had shown, this raging beast, and it destroyed everything. They became stranded on a planet that corresponded with nothing they had ever seen, lost somewhere in space as virtual prisoners. Their radio equipment torn off and left somewhere on the battle fields of Europe and only a beacon to signal to C.A.K.E. that they were still alive.

This beast symbolised that helplessness, the captivity, and now here it was and he could see it held Alice in one hand and the native in the other. Prisoners again, and he was not prepared to fall foul of that same fate. He had a chance to escape so he turned and ran.

Blight now had his hands full. The figures he had grasped squirmed and wriggled but he gripped them tightly so much of his work for the Prince was done. He now just had to destroy, to make a point that you did not, could not, escape the Prince.

The figure ran for the trees, but with one sweep of its forearm the blight swept the trees away.

Byron had made his escape from the path. He

would find the river and Harmony himself and be safe from the beast, but the trees were torn from the ground and broken off around him. They crashed down and splinters tore at his clothes and flesh. He had stumbled to the ground, pinned by a heavy branch across his legs, so he rolled, scrabbled for freedom but in turning he saw the beast above him with its cold dead eyes and the crying face of his wife held in its grip as it lifted a foot to crush all life from his cowardly heart.

Harmony tore across the tree tops and struck the beast hard in the temple. The effect was impressive; the creature, balanced on just one leg, went flying backwards as if it had been struck by the punch of an equally titanic foe. The Harmony, not designed for impacts spun off at a weird angle, barrelling over itself as it clipped the tree tops. Blight crashed down hard, its hands opening from the impact and throwing it's captives free, to roll across the devastated ground.

Byron couldn't understand what had happened but he realised he had been given a second chance. He was up and on his feet but instead of the safety of the trees he ran towards the beast, grabbed his wife's hand and had her up on her feet. Together they were everything, she was the voice and the action, and he was the brain. Byron could not survive without his Alice, and fear had almost made him give her up. Together they ran away from the beast not sure if it would recover before they escaped, but willing to take the chance.

Scarlett stood too. She was the far side of the Titan, closer the Menhune village than escape. Harmony was flying and she could only believe that Crash was behind the controls, despite all logic that pointed towards the contrary. Before her the beast started to rise, it had a wound to its head and looked dazed but as it stood she could see it was looking for the couple she had promised to save with Crash. She couldn't allow it. On the ground was a broken branch, not too heavy, but sharp and reasonably straight. She lifted it up, gauged its balance and let fly.

It didn't stick into the creature far, it caused it very little pain but it certainly got its attention. The Blight turned its sickly eyes towards Scarlett and roared.

She ran back down the hill and after a brief pause while the creature assessed her worth, it gave chase and moved away from the fleeing Futurenauts.

***

On the courtyard the Persians had watched with interest, as the Titan had raged and shown its anger. Then it was struck, floored by an

Welcome to Jahannam

unknown object, a projectile from the jungle. Corvus had run forward but now his titan was running back and they could all see it pursued a woman towards them. Soon she was stood on the lip of the abyss.

Before her stood the Persian metal men raising their weapons barring her way, behind her the great beast came to a halt. It raised its colossal hand to grab her when Corvus shouted "KILL HER!"

With this the hand turned to a deadly fist and struck downwards, but again Harmony came. Crash flew his ship straight at the back of the beasts head, hitting the cranium hard and bouncing off towards the sky. The impact only moved the Titan a fraction but the momentum of its downward strike carried it off the Apergy and into the great Abyss before it, where it fell headfirst and roaring into the darkness below. Corvus was on his hands and knees watching his beast fall to its doom; his chance to wrestle the crown from his father gone. He looked up with anger and there alone on the far ledge was Scarlett.

"You're mine." He hissed, and pulling a slim bladed sword from his side he approached the unarmed girl across one of the smaller bridges of the abyss. He only turned to the soldiers once. "If it looks for a second like she will win, kill her." Corvus had not survived his warring siblings and maniacal father by making headstrong decisions, every plan had an escape.

Scarlett watched the Prince approach, his light silk clothes flapping in the wind from the Abyss pressing against his skeletal frame, his benign ceramic face seeming to leer as he swished his sword through the air, its perfect craftsmanship making it cut the air with a tuneful hiss.

She had nothing but she stood her ground. Then she felt a familiar weight in her boot and stooping, she pulled forth her father's bayonet. A knife that had saved her on so many an occasion, overlooked by the guards on her capture and forgotten by her in the unfolding excitement.

As she stood brandishing the blade, Corvus let out a derisive laugh but said no more. He had the extended reach, her blade would make her foolhardy but it also meant he could toy with her.

He struck out with his blade and she turned it aside with ease, he struck again and once again she turned it aside. He paced around her, she followed his movements so the troops and abyss were at her back, then he thrust. She took a step back but turned the attack aside. Corvus loved this, he couldn't decide if he should run her through or force her down after his Titan. He thrust, Scarlett forced his blade down and lunged forward, her fist striking the Prince full

Welcome to Jahannam

in the face. It sent him flying and behind her she heard a series of rifles brought to bear on her back.

But the prince shot up his hand to hold them and no volley came.

He stood slowly and when he turned again to face her she could see her blow had shattered his mask from the top lip down, he wiped at his face and the broken bottom fell away revealing the skull beneath full of swirling mist.

"You can't kill me girl. I am immortal. I gave up woundable flesh before your mother gave in to the sins of hers."

Scarlett almost roared as she charged but the sting in her side stopped her dead. She looked down to feel the bloom of pain radiate through her as it opened its blood red petals. Corvus laughed at how she had impaled herself and started to pull his blade free from the flesh.

"No, you don't get to die now. I want to dance some more." He said, and even without lips Scarlett could hear the smile in his voice. She plunged herself back onto his blade. It had not been a mistake the first time, but a way of forcing his hand, holding his weapon, reducing the damage he could do. As she pushed forward it went deeper, through her body, and she grabbed the Prince by his shoulder and spun him over the abyss.

"You may kill me but if I throw you into the glimmer you know these bones, your bones, will be lost. Pulverised by the fall. Without a body you become just mist. I don't know much of your royal line but I know enough to know without substance you become just another citizen of your fathers, you lose your royal bonds." Scarlett smiled. In a game of chess she had sacrificed her queen to kill the king. It would have been at this point that the soldiers would have fired, killed her and sent them tumbling into the abyss and devastation for them both. However, Crash had gained control of Harmony again and for a third and final time, he did what he did best and crashed with style. He tore up the courtyard beside the abyss and tore through the Persian troops, rending metal in twain and casting those closest the edge into the abyss. The impact threw Scarlett and Corvus back from the pit in a great painful heap as a cloud of dust and detritus rained down.

It took Scarlett a couple of seconds to recover but when she did she was alone, the blade still through her. With great pain and through gritted teeth she pulled it free. Corvus must have been running and she saw he was back across the bridge and climbing the steps, calling at his remaining soldiers as he did to either follow him or cover his retreat.

Crash forced himself from the broken Harmony. She was in a bad way but he thought her fixable with time. He practically fell from her skirt and suddenly was in a hail of weapons

Welcome to Jahannam

fire. The soldiers had not been on the courtyard alone, more were positioned up the terraces guarding the homes of imprisoned Menhune. He was pinned down, but around him were the guns of the fallen Persians. He grabbed one and was glad its design was like an ancient flintlock in appearance, so it was simply aim and fire. As he was aiming Scarlett dived in beside him, both using Harmony for cover.

"You certainly turn up when needed." She smiled picking up another fallen rifle. "Ignore the soldiers on the steps and shoot the guards, let's see if we can free some angry Menhune." Crash liked her thinking. He aimed and shot at the guards. It certainly took a few bullets to take them down but the bullets glowed as they flew and you could see how good your aim was and adjust accordingly. As predicted, the battle was soon being joined by the Menhune. The diminutive warriors seemed to be armed more primitively than the Persians but they were fighting hard and the forces of the metal men were depleting and falling fast.

Corvus had made it to the top house. He was cursing but had taken a few soldiers with him. "I have lost everything." He shouted in rage " I must escape with at least my bones." He turned around looking for a weapon in case the defences fell, when his eyes landed on the table at which Byron had been writing all evening.

He snatched up the parchment and read quickly. When he next spoke he was calmer. "Maybe we have at least come away with a prize. " he turned to his soldiers "Loose your shells and bear me up."

Without question the mists left the armoured bodies which crumpled like discarded puppets, as the smoke that was the Persians' true form surrounded the bones of their Prince. With so many retainers the Prince flew into the air and like a skilled bird of prey dived out through the hole in the wall and away across the trees, his clothes flapping like dark wings.

Welcome to Jahannam

Epilogue

The futurenauts stood on the courtyard of the Menhune village. The cavorite sphere had been pulled down to rest securely on the tidied stones. Alice smiled at Crash as Byron stood by the sphere making his final checks.

"Are you sure you won't come with us?" She asked again.

"I'm sure. The Sphere only takes two comfortably, three is a push. It's a bit of a long journey to not have comfort." He glanced across at Byron before continuing "I promised Scarlett could come back with me so I need to stay here and fix Harmony. If you follow my instructions you'll be back on Earth in about four months which is long before I'll have her ready to fly again."

"And you're sure we can take your spare radio? We know what it's like to be stranded here and not reach home." Alice asked, concerned.

Crash laughed "I'm not going to be far behind you, I promise. I doubt the main radio will break before then. You heard how well it worked when you spoke to your mother."

Alice smiled. "I know you're right, I'm just worried for you."

Crash looked at Scarlett. "I'm pretty sure we'll be fine." He held out his hand. "I think we're delaying Byron's launch window."

Alice looked back at her husband who wore his practiced look of impatience, before turning back to Crash and shaking his hand.

"He means well. He just likes to be closer to home." Alice smiled at Scarlett "Thank you for everything, we'll make sure you have a warm welcome when you come to Earth. Look after him until then."

Scarlett was looking at the sphere, concerned, beside it she could see the wreck of Harmony and although Crash had convinced her it was just a few dents she was unsure the Futurenauts were not all just being headstrong and over confident in their repair skills. "And you're sure your vessel is repaired and you don't want to wait for us? I mean Crash knows the way and we'd all be together."

"He's given us very clear instructions. We'll be fine, but thank you for the concern." Alice paused for a moment and then embraced Scarlett. "Thank you again."

With this Alice turned and joined her husband.
There was waving, and soon Byron and Alice had disappeared inside and started their interior checks before launch.
***
Even the Menhune stopped what they were doing to watch the sphere leave. Scarlett looked at Harmony.

Welcome to Jahannam

"Are you sure you can fix her?" Crash smiled back at her.

"Eventually. My mission was to get them safely off the planet and on their way home. I've done that but I also promised I'd get you to Earth and I couldn't have done that if I had gone with them." Scarlett beamed

"Thank you Crash Jackson."

"Besides I can speak to the Menhune now. " He tapped the polyglot on his neck. "And knowing both Corvus and the Titan he corrupted both escaped. I couldn't possibly leave until we make sure they are safe from a revenge attack."

Scarlett looked up at Crash with hooded eyes and a pout "And is that the only thing you can think of doing while you remain here?"

Crash smiled softly "Well I could always get to know the residents of Jahannam better." With those words he wrapped his arm around her waist and pulled her closer. Their lips met in passion.

***

"What do you mean Earthman?" The cloaked figure stood by the large circular window surveying his kingdom, the light beyond threw him almost entirely into silhouette, so just flashes of his red apparel could be seen. "The planet is crawling in

Earthmen, they are a plague."

The courtier who had been tasked with bringing the news looked at the Kings privy counselor who nodded

"The Earthman didn't come by storm my King. He travelled here in a craft." The courtier almost whispered, his form now so prostrate his wooden head was touching the floor.

"Portal?" the King asked his powerful voice stretching out the word.

"No my King, from the stars." The Privy counselor interjected, feeling the news should come from a less wavering voice.

The figure at the window turned slightly and the room fell even more silent. Awaiting the Kings words

"Find him and bring him and his craft here. Kill anyone who gets in your way."

"Prince Corvus, my King?" The Privy counselor enquired again, less sure that the beginning part of the Courtiers message had been remembered, aware of the weight of what the King was saying.

The King turned on his counselor, the sculpted glass dome that was his head contained nothing but swirling mist and a blackened skull. When he spoke again, his voice was clear and

Welcome to Jahannam

purposeful.

"Anyone who gets in your way."